BOOK ONE IN
THE BOUND SERIES

Forever Bound

CHLOE STOWE

For more information contact:
Riverdale Avenue Books
5676 Riverdale Avenue
Riverdale, NY 10471
www.riverdaleavebooks.com

Design by www.formatting4U.com
Cover by Scott Carpenter
Digital ISBN: 978-1-62601-382-7
Print ISBN: 978-1-62601-383-4

First Edition, February 2010, Ravenous Romance
Second edition, June 2017

Author's Notes

The first two works of the *Forever Bound* series take place before the repeal of the United States Military's DADT (Don't Ask, Don't Tell) policy. During this time, openly gay, lesbian or bisexual individuals were prohibited from serving their country in any of the Armed Forces. Like an axe, this regulation hung over all who chose to follow their hearts over outdated regulations. The atmosphere for these soldiers was one of secrecy and constant fear of being "discovered." This policy was finally repealed in late 2011.

Chapter One

Playgrounds

Floodlights lit the night sky. Mosquitoes buzzing here and there accompanied the *thud...thud...swish!* of the basketball game. The two men were playing one on one. Sweat poured down both of their faces, and grunts and curses rattled off the side of the house. The net was torn and hung lopsided from the dark red rim. It blew in the gulf breeze as the two men scrambled for the loose ball.

"Foul!" Aaron Chambers yelled as he crashed into the ground. He was becoming well acquainted with the patio and its attractive but painful cement. He figured a few of its newer cracks had to be credited to him and his ass tonight. Levering himself up on what was now his good elbow, Aaron swore that the next time John invited him over for a beer and steaks, he was ditching the sweats and T-shirt and kitting out in full combat gear. Maybe even bring his gun. "You getting up?" A sneer from the perpetrator above interrupted his thoughts of sweet revenge.

Clutching his freshly skinned elbow in his hand, Aaron glared accusingly up at the man who was

1

supposed to be his best friend, not to mention his occasional lover. The occasional part was going to become a hell of a lot more pronounced if John didn't stand down from kill-mode.

Aaron had known John Castle for nine years. He'd been fucking him for five. He had been more or less in love with the bastard for three. Guess it was about time for one of them to kill the other.

It was even odds as to who would win.

Usually, it was a fairly even match between the men. Both were in their early thirties, John a year older, and both were tremendously fit. John cycled. Aaron ran. Both swam miles in John's pool every week, but that was where the similarities drifted out of sight and vanished altogether.

Aaron had golden brown hair, chocolate eyes, lightly tanned skin, and while he could most likely kill you with his pinkie, he was much more likely to kill you with his grin.

John was dark-haired, fair-skinned, and had green eyes the color of rain-washed moss. He used his extra inch or so of height to intimidate those he couldn't simply outthink. In the end, few men noticed how tall he was.

Gulping several lungfuls of hot summer air, John looked down at his scowling opponent and the wounded arm held piteously out for inspection. He quickly diagnosed the problem. "Crybaby."

"I'm bleeding here." Aaron pointed to a scratch that was going to get more gruesome when he shoved said elbow through John's smirk any second now.

Scoffing at Aaron's antics, John tossed the hard-won basketball between his hands. "Suck it up. Unless I see bone, I don't want to hear it."

"Fine." Aaron pulled himself painfully up. "The paramedics can fill you in."

"Sure," John shrugged, then with a wink added, "Right after…"

Swoosh! went the ball effortlessly through the hoop.

Aaron could only shake his head. Whatever was going on in his friend's head tonight was damned irritating. "You're a bastard, you know that?"

"Learned from the master." John tossed the retrieved ball back to the losing side with a snide smile.

"Sweet-talking me, Doctor?" Aaron forced a chuckle, as he tucked the basketball up safely under his arm and out of the reach of any roaming big-brained maniacs. "You lose a busload of orphans on the table today?"

"Ass," John muttered as he turned to the patio table and the warm bottle of beer it still held for him.

It was rare for John to drink, rarer still for him to drink beer. He was more a top-shelf kind of a guy these days; his propensity for beer guzzling vanished after a particular memorable weekend many years ago. Putting all the warning signs together, Aaron was getting a sick feeling in his gut. Knowing that things had a habit of getting uglier before they got better, he pasted on a smile and joined the good surgeon at the table for a swig of his own beer. "That's *Colonel* Ass to you," Aaron impatiently reminded. "Or do I have to get my wings out again?"

John snorted.

Aaron expected as much. John could never quite believe that the Air Force had not only kept Aaron around all these years, but kept on promoting him, too.

Frankly, Aaron didn't get it either, but it was a fucked-up world. The pilot figured he might as well ride the madness until the end.

"So?" Aaron prompted as he bumped his friend's shoulder. "You going to tell me, or just let it eat at you?" John was a hell of a good orthopedic surgeon; his reputation was golden and well earned. Not much rattled him.

John blew out a shaky breath and reluctantly gave it up. "Cerebral aneurysm ruptured as I was closing up."

It was usually something like that. Something his friend, or any doctor for that matter, would have no control over. John, though, liked to wring all the guilt he could out of this kind of situation. "Sorry," Aaron voiced aloud, all the while letting his insides curse up a hell of a storm at the world and its cackling fates. He'd love to give those three bitches a chuckle or two himself.

John busied himself scraping the label off the beer bottle with his thumbnail. It was a focusing tactic Aaron knew well. Experience had taught him to just stand back and let John's oversized brain turn things over and over, and eventually the inevitable gem of wisdom would tumble out.

This time it was a very tiny rock.

"Life," John lamented with soulless green eyes. With that monologue complete, he swallowed down the last of his beer with a noticeable grimace and disappeared back into silence.

Aaron would have been dumbstruck if he wasn't so freaking aggravated. Deep thoughts were supposed to be falling out of his lover's mouth, not cryptic silence. Hell, if John was going to play the strong and

4

silent type, Aaron might as well dive right in and see what the loud and annoying type could shake loose. "As in… 'Life's a bitch?' 'Life's a box of sour cherries?'" he suggested, trying desperately to drag his friend at least out of monosyllables. "Or better yet, how about an oldie but a goodie… 'Life sucks'?"

Green eyes met brown and warned of nothing less than desperation. "Yeah," John agreed in a low, graveled voice. "Life sucks, but you know what? Death sucks more." Like an old, broken man, John turned and slowly headed back to their makeshift playground of ball and cement.

Insight hit Aaron like a ball-peen hammer to the knee.

"It's the wrong playground." Aaron cursed himself. He had been an idiot not to see it before.

Leaning tiredly against the side of his house, John asked with a frown, "What'd you say?"

The idea was a calculated risk, but Aaron loved the fool and trusted him more than he did any other soul on this Earth. John needed reminding of that tonight. This would say it all. With a little twinge of excitement in his gut, Aaron headed straight over to John. Shoving the basketball hard into the man's chest, Aaron demanded, "Put me down, John."

"No." The answer was quick and not unexpected. John was anything but easy.

"Come on! Do it." Aaron wasn't beyond being an ass to get his way. "You need the control. Take it."

"What? Here?" At the nod, John added emphatically, "No fucking way." He started to walk away.

"Chicken! Should I cluck for you?" Aaron shouted at his back.

"Well, you are the one with wings, *Colonel*," John turned and fired back.

"Shut up!" Aaron seethed, stepping right into the man's sneering face. Shoving his finger hard into John's chest with each word, he dared, "Make. Me. Shut. Up."

John shoved Aaron away, and he hit hard against the side of the house. Forcing himself to take a step back, John shook with a barely contained fury as he warned, "Do you have *any* idea what I could do to you tonight?"

Slowly, deliberately taunting him, Aaron curled his lips into a cocky smile. "Come on, Doc, you know I'd beat you down."

"Shut up!" John growled and rammed Aaron back into the wall again. His forearm held hard and unmoving across Aaron's chest.

Aaron laughed, knowing it would only take one more push. A cruel one. "All talk, no action. No wonder you couldn't save…"

With a roar of utter ferocity, John grabbed the back of Aaron's neck, stared the laughing boy dead in the eye and said, "Fucking fall for me, pet!"

* * *

Subspace. It was a playground they had rarely played in, and never without the supervision of those more experienced. Private dungeons in private clubs in far-off cities had been their only option. With Aaron's career and the small-minded rules that governed it, they could never be too careful. While BDSM had always been a part of their sexual relationship, they had only recently experienced this extreme. It had taken work and absolute trust to be granted entrance into such a precious realm.

They had never explored it alone.

That virginity would end tonight.

* * *

Oblivion took Aaron without a whimper.

Propping the suddenly weakened body up against the wall, John drank in the sight of submission swallowing a man whole.

Already, Aaron looked well and truly fucked, and put to bed still hard. Tottering before John like a puppet on a drunken man's string, Aaron was a living, breathing wet dream. His whole body thrummed in sultry, unconscious movement. Deep, shuddering breaths riddled his chest, sending strained aftershocks rocking through his abs. His thighs and calves and ass muscles trembled as they bore the weight of a cock throbbing to fullness as it was stunned awake. His lips hung slightly parted, his face was flushed. Slowly, almost imperceptibly, his head rocked from side to side against the house. What little focus his gaze still had was locked unerringly on John, silently begging the man for more words.

"Dropping feels so good, doesn't it?" John expected and received no answer from the stunned man. With long, soft strokes, he petted back Aaron's hair, adding to the hypnotic rhythm of Aaron's smooth and measured fall.

"Drop all the way down," John cooed, the hint of steel he wielded he kept contained in his eyes for now. The descent needed to be eased into its completion, like soft feathers cushioning a man's fall. "Let it all go and just drift for me. Drift far away and into me."

Aaron's dark brown eyes fought the urge to roll up and disappear into the back of his head.

Adrenaline pounded through John's veins. The rush of power in watching this soldier crumble within the palms of John's hands was an exhilaration nothing short of orgasmic. The empowerment was unspeakable, to know the same hands that had lost a woman in the prime of her life today, the same hands that had failed so miserably just hours ago, now reigned absolutely.

And all John wanted was more.

It was that primal hunger for power that destroyed any doubts John might have harbored, and any inhibitions he might have held.

In that singular moment, John truly became Master.

Cupping the wavering Aaron's face in his hand, John trailed his thumb across his mouth as he commanded, "Your mouth, these gorgeous lips, won't speak again. Not a sound, not a whimper. Total silence, my pet, or you will be hooded. If you understand, nod once for me."

There was one nod.

"Strip." John let go, stepped back, and watched.

Achingly slowly, Aaron rid himself of his clothes. It was uncoordinated, unbalanced, and sexy as fucking hell.

Aaron had a magnificent body. All long, lean lines sculpted in smooth, hard muscle. His cock was textbook beauty nestled in sandy brown curls. Half-risen, it awaited command, the pre-come weeping from its tip the only sign of its impatience.

Finally, with eyes black in dazed lust, Aaron stood naked, swaying gently in the breeze. John could feast himself on this vision for a lifetime, but being the bastard he was, he again wanted more.

"Present yourself."

A switch was thrown somewhere deep inside Aaron's inner workings. One second he was malleable putty struggling to stand, the next he was a soldier frozen at rigid attention. Legs and ankles were bound together by rote. Naked toes pointed outward at precise 45-degree angles. Fingers were curled inward to the body, their tips ghosting bare thighs. Elbows and knees were slightly bent, while eyes blank and unmoving stared straight ahead. His whole body seemed to lean forward. No commander could ask more of any minion.

Pleased, John circled the shell that once was his lover Aaron. Every muscle of the statue was taut; the frozen shell hardly seemed to be breathing. "Just as it should be," John spoke to the night. "Obedient and dumb." For the rest of the charmed, darkened hours, Aaron Chambers would be nothing more than a body—a body John now owned and controlled outright.

John Castle nearly came in his fucking pants.

The body simply stood at attention.

"Arch position!" John suddenly barked, a cruel smile twisting his lips.

The position was a simple one: to literally bend over backwards. Only feet and palms would be holding up the bowed body, leaving the penis as an erect offering on an altar of skin.

The incredible thing about a soldier was his flexibility. It wasn't expected. It awed.

In the middle of their makeshift court, Aaron lay down on his back. With hands beside his head, fingers pointed to shoulders, effortlessly it seemed, he raised himself up and into position.

John nearly drooled as he inspected his good boy.

Long, tanned toes strained as they dug into the cement, buttressing the taut bow of the bare, trembling body. In the light of the fair Florida moon, the tiny beads of sweat bejeweled the long, smooth stretches of skin. The tip of John's forefinger ghosted across the tortuously twisting trails of these gems. The skin shivered in the touch's wake. The subtle dance of muscles as the body breathed, quickened, spasmed, then went out of step. The toes clenched tighter. The bow threatened to break.

"It's not easy, is it, pet?" John bent down and whispered in an ear. "Staying so still, so quiet, while your Master does this." A pert, brown nipple was pinched, twisted, pulled and released.

"Or blows on that." A hot breath blew across balls.

"Or bites this." Teeth clamped down and nibbled greedily on the abused, now fiery red nipple.

The body did not even quiver.

"Good boy." John dropped a chaste kiss on the offered navel.

Again, neither a shiver nor a shudder.

"My boy gets a reward," with a punishingly slow deliberation, John drew his tongue down a line from his pet's collarbone to his hipbone. He studied the skin as he journeyed across the body. Every pore, every rib, every muscle John memorized for later engagements in this delicious playground of theirs.

As the cusp of the hip was reached, a long, painfully aroused mewl escaped from the back of the body's throat.

John immediately pulled away. "What was that? Was that a noise?" A devilish smile looked down at the now feverishly trembling body. "Yes, I think it was a noise." With an open-handed uppercut at lightning speed, John hit Aaron's ass.

Hard.

Ten times, the firm, quivering cheeks were mercilessly punished.

Not a noise was made. Only the strained bobbing of an Adam's apple counted the lashings.

"Better," John growled as a hungry gleam grew in his eyes. He knew neither man would last much longer. In greedy anticipation of the feast about to come, he slowly licked his lips, announcing proudly, "Now, it's time for Master's reward."

Laid out before him on a buffet of gently quivering skin, John's meal awaited him with an anxious twitch. Straining out of its nest of musky brown curls, the cock rose to meet its Master's lips. Ever so gently, John cradled the shaft's head within his warm mouth and against his still tongue. For long seconds of no movement but breath, he held the treasure inside him. The taste, the bitter warm tang of the tender skin on a roughened tongue was reward enough for John's senses, but the Master in his subconscious craved more.

John nipped Aaron's foreskin with his careful but hungry teeth.

The gargle of gentled pain was allowed.

Like a cat with its lips firmly encasing a canary,

the Master grinned around the captured cock. It was time for dinner.

Quickly, the rhythm of the encounter intensified.

Master deep-throated the penis, sucking its every exposed pore.

Two fingers jutted upwards into the reddened, punished ass and immediately penetrated its hot, hidden hole.

Aaron's body bucked than buckled.

John tightened his teeth around writhing meat as warning.

The body bolted back up, knees and elbows locked again in position.

John laughed around the throated cock, then went in for the kill.

In an assault both merciless and devastating, pleasure was literally wrung out of the pet's body. The prostate was found. It was hit. It was stroked. It was hit again. Again.

The orgasm was inevitable, and ripped through Aaron's body in catastrophic wave after wave.

The Master milked his pet with wanton abandon. Not a drop of come remained in Aaron's body as he finally crumpled unconscious into his lover's arms.

John came with a scream and cried.

* * *

The shudders of the spent orgasm slowly ceased, abating into only a delicious memory that John would gather around his shoulders when the world turned cold.

John Castle was warm most days. The passion he

had for his career burned brighter every day, it seemed. He lived for the lives he had a hand in saving, and he saved most. There were those, however, whom he lost, like the poor woman today. It was those lost lives, the ones whisked away without warning, without giving him a fair chance to fight for them, that chilled him to the core.

It was in that cold that he doubted. It was in that cold that he panicked. It was in that cold that John knew he had no control.

Closer, tighter, he held Aaron to his chest. It was this control that Aaron had gifted him tonight—had forced down his throat, literally. How could a soul feel anything but warm holding such a heart in his arms?

John looked down at the sleeping face. Aaron would wake in the morning his usual S.O.B. self, but until then the spent bastard was simply angelic. John softly laughed at the absurdity of their lives and their love. He whispered into the sweat-soaked brown hair, "My angel with fighter pilot wings."

* * *

In the bushes that lay hidden in the shadows of their playground, a pair of hateful eyes stared.

Only to him were the two gunshots not a surprise.

Chapter Two

Iron

John had planted the bushes for Aaron. He remembered distinctly standing in Panama City's largest nursery with a world of horticultural delights laid out before them only to have Aaron insist on roses for the side yard of John's brand-new house.

"Roses?" John had asked with a decidedly surprised tweak to his voice.

"Colorado," Aaron had answered simply. "Colorado grows gorgeous roses. Bet you didn't know that."

"No, I didn't. Why do I know that now?"

"Reminds me of home, and since, well, I was kind of hoping I could think of your new place as a back-up home… you know, if my condo gets blown away or falls in the ocean or something. It was just a thought, a stupid thought, but…"

John had held up his hand, begging for the rambling to stop. Once he had Aaron's attention and silence, John had stated unequivocally, "Not pink."

The smile that had immediately lit Aaron's face, John knew, would be well worth a lifetime of thorns.

14

John had rolled his eyes at his own thought, but still manned up and headed for the rose section.

Aaron had fallen in happily beside him, scoffing easily at John's concern. "Of course not pink roses, Doctor. White roses to go with your yellow house."

Now, John screwed up his face and squinted into the dark of his yard. Blades of grass obstructed his view. "What the hell?" he grumbled as he touched a growing lump at the back of his head. "How did I..." He tried to sit up but found a dead weight holding him down. The world was having trouble regaining its proper focus, so he was squinting again as he looked down at his chest and the dead—

"Oh, God." The two gunshots, the spray of blood, the momentum of two bullets sending John's head hard into the pavement—all of it came flooding back as Aaron's motionless body sprawled across his own came into sharp focus.

John acted quickly and intelligently, his medical training bullying its way past the shock. It was a blur: moving Aaron's hemorrhaging body to the blood-slicked patio, the stuttering taps to the phone's nine and one, the finding and slow counting of his best friend's pulse, the finding and slow counting of bullet holes in his best friend's body.

"Two," John croaked out to the moon. "Head and chest." There were more technically exact words for the injuries but his mind was quickly regressing to the basics. The basics were bad enough.

A lazy breeze brought with it the scent of roses.

"White roses," John mumbled as he pushed the blood back into his lover's body. "White roses to go with my yellow house."

15

As John's mind wound back to the beginning, to the day they met nine years ago, the would-be assassin stole silently away from the sea of white roses...

* * *

It was a classic football Saturday in the South. Tailgating with 100,000 of your closest friends, trading homebrewed beer for slow-cooked wings, cursing and cheering the goal-line gods in the same breath—it was the womb where 23-old medical student John Castle had become a man. Having finally sprung up his last inches of height the past year, John could now claim six feet and two inches as his own. While an embarrassingly late bloomer in height, John had been able to hold the title of handsome for all of his life. Thick, luxurious tufts of dark brown hair had followed him from birth, making him a perpetual favorite for holding and snuggling. Although he now wore his hair cut fairly short, he did keep enough of its length for a well-tossed wind to brush attractively over a random brow. Brushing the stray lock off of his face was a nervous habit he rarely allowed himself to practice. He was in much more control than that.

That image of a self-disciplined, well-manicured doctor that he tried so hard most days to portray, however, was taking a beating this afternoon, and John simply didn't care. Sprawled out in an old lawn chair, his feet crossed on a beat-up cooler, John soaked up the rare lazy moment with a hungry relish.

Late autumn had kissed the dying leaves with burnt oranges and scorching reds. The deep blue of the noon sky carried on its breezes a welcome warmth that took the bite out of the chill November air. A rousing buzz of fight songs, car horns, and sports radio thrummed everywhere. It was electric, and so bursting with a life all its own, John didn't feel a need to add anything. Simply *being* seemed enough for today.

"And drinking," he added wryly to himself as he cracked open his second beer of the day. "Drinking and being. That's it for today."

No argument came against this mighty declaration, simply for the fact that no one else was there. For the blessed moment, John had this little patch of Auburn, Alabama, all to himself. Oh, he could see the mass of humanity streaming by at the end of the gravel driveway, but the row of weathered-iron fence posts that surrounded the century-old house kept even the strangest of strangers at bay.

The house sat crookedly in the middle of its one-quarter acre of land, facing a strange little corner that held a freakishly tall elm tree and a stone bench that lay split down its center. Clapboards once painted white, now a dingy gray, clung loosely to all but one side of the house. A long, wooden porch that swayed in its middle sat perched like a funhouse mask across the little dwelling's face. Incongruously, the lawn was perfectly mowed and not a weed rose from any of its dormant flowerbeds.

The house was a far from welcoming spot, with its only attribute seeming to be its location, a handful of blocks from the college town's center, Toomer's Corner. With the house torn down and the land cleared, John was sure the lot could sell for a handsome price. Apparently the Tasker family clung to this place fiercely. One of these days, he really needed to ask Liam the story behind this odd little house. As John stuffed the last bite of hot dog into his mouth, he chuckled to himself. "Yeah, right after our next fuck I'll be sure to bring it up."

John Castle and Liam Tasker had been lovers for six months. They had met at the University of Florida in a physiology class they both abhorred. Abhorrence led to a drink after a particularly miserable exam, and the drink to some on-hands appeasement at Liam's off-campus dorm. Admittedly there had been little talk that first night, but the second and third nights had clued them in that they might really like one another— beyond the sweaty sheets. Neither kidded themselves that true love was involved. Truth be told, they enjoyed being part of a couple more than they enjoyed being with one another. Medical school could be a lonely place when you actually cared about being the best, and John and Liam both fought tooth and nail to be that top dog. So it was this mixture of convenience, mutual respect, and a shared physical attraction for each other that had kept the men pleasantly satisfied the last half year, and had brought John here to this odd little house peeking out from a row of iron spikes. "Damn," John lamented far too sourly for his own taste." I wish there was some whiskey."

In fact, that was where Liam was at the moment, a last-minute liquor-and-chips run. With traffic basically at a standstill and the sidewalks cluttered with oversized RVs and pop-up souvenir stands, it wasn't going to be a quick errand. He'd been gone an hour and would probably be gone at least an hour more. John felt a little guilty for not going with him, but Liam had played the so-called "you're-our-guest" card. So he had been relegated to keep the Tasker family homestead secure from the more obnoxious of the game day claim-jumpers, as Dwight Tasker liked to call them. John shook his head, still surprised that Liam's old man didn't leave him with a gun and a load of buckshot to deal with the alleged vermin. Liam's family were a bit old school, hence the intense downplaying of John and Liam's extracurricular activities the last few days. John made no argument, as he saw no need to rock the boat when he was swimming around in borrowed waters. John snorted at his choice of words. "Shit, I'm starting to talk like them, too."

Rethinking the whole drinking-and-being idea as maybe leaning a bit far towards honest retrospection, John grabbed the bill of his ball cap and tugged it down over his dark green eyes. Stretching his sweater-clad arms back behind his head, John mused aloud, "What the hell am I doing here?"

"Was just asking myself the same question." A stranger's voice arrived on a particularly warm breath of wind.

Praying that a stray member of Liam's clan hadn't just wandered in from the proverbial fields, John lifted up his cap and cracked open an eye. What he saw was a vision.

Leaning over the iron gate of the driveway, a man with the quirkiest smile and the most delicious body awaited John's gaze. With thighs clad in tight blue jeans that occasionally disappeared into a most-welcoming, revealing tear, John could barely coax his eyes away from these windows of honey-colored skin. A thin white T-shirt covered a hardly concealed six-pack of abs. Although a weathered brown leather jacket hid the full extent of their glory, John didn't begrudge the coat its presence, as it hung a distinctive air of ruggedness onto the broad shoulders. Deep golden blond hair covered the man's head in a stylish military cut. Dark sunglasses hid his eyes, but the strong jawbone, the high cheekbones, and the full, soft lips curling into a devil-may-care grin did more than hint at an extraordinarily alluring face.

The beer can nearing catastrophic meltdown in John's viselike grip creaked out in loud disapproval of the manhandling and thankfully brought the doctor out of his fugue. Quickly replaying the entirety of their conversation in a nanosecond or two, he located the right words. "So, uh, got an answer?" he stuttered.

"Nope. You?" Somehow the man's grin blossomed all the more.

John doubted he could take much more. Pushing himself out of the safety of the lawn chair's confines, he took his very interested cock closer, venturing slowly and oh-so-casually to the gate. Once there, he smirked with a confident lack of drool. "Not a damn clue."

Oblivious to the way his body danced across the keys of John's libido, the stranger took a step back and rattled the locked gate wryly. "At least I'm on the right side of these bars."

A block away, an air horn blast immediately cut through the air. While the man at the gate didn't so much as flinch, he did take a wary look around his surroundings. The cow bell that suddenly began to clang a house down only added to John's enjoyment in saying, "You sure about that?"

"No." Aaron laughed, and with a casual sweep of his hand, took off his sunglasses and graced John's world with his eyes. Toasty brown, they burned in a deep rich earthiness, both primal and mesmerizing. John didn't know whether to stare or just leap dick first into their promised warmth. In the end, he simply nudged open the door with two words and a surprisingly steady hand. "John Castle."

With a grip firm and welcoming, the stranger had a name. "Aaron Chambers."

"Care for a beer?" John offered, mainly to give his body something innocent to do.

"Said the spider to the fly." Blowing back a cobweb dangling from the fencepost that kept tickling the end of his nose, Aaron laughed.

John joined him. "I think they call it atmosphere."

"They?" Aaron quirked his left brow at the solitary man.

John almost said, "my lover's family," but caught himself just in time. He had made Liam a promise and was going to keep it. "Some old family friends of mine."

"Ahh." Aaron nodded slowly, giving the place another wary look-see.

"Yeah, well, distant family friends." John enunciated that key word firmly.

"No need to explain." The corner of his lips curled gently in amusement, "You should see the crew I'm with."

"They got a nice set of iron bars too?"

Holding up his finger in agreement, Aaron granted with a smile, "Point."

"Here!" John tossed a beer to this new

acquaintance. "Have a cold one, flyboy," he said, referring to the USAF emblazoned across Aaron's shirt.

Aaron eyed him. "I'm thinking full-time student, something heady. Law?"

Amused, John looked down at himself. A pair of dark gray jeans sat comfortably on his hips with old leatherwork boots peeking out from their hem. A cream-colored sweater that had seen better days, if not years, completed the scholarly look. John shook his head, amazed Aaron could make the leap from his current state of scruffiness to a shockingly close guess. "Med school," he corrected.

"Not enough of those around." A teasing spark burned gently in Aaron's eyes.

Tweaked nicely by the unexpected volley, John sent one of his own, all wrapped up in old-timer's Southern twang. "Somebody's got to clean up you boys' messes."

Aaron laughed outright. "Thanks, *Grandpa*."

"Young whippersnapper!" John honestly didn't know where that came from, but suspected that Liam's family somehow had a hand in it.

Aaron, for his part, snorted a good portion of his beer right out his nose. Cleaning up the mess he'd made as best he could amidst red-cheeked snickers, he admitted, "I haven't done that since the fourth grade."

A genuine grin that felt sadly foreign to his lips graced John's face. "Bet there's some paper towels inside, but I'm not going in there by myself." John unlocked and swung open the creaky gate. "Got your gun?"

"Don't need it." Aaron strode purposefully in, a

twinkle in the brown of his eyes. "I've got a doctor to lob between me and any trouble."

John stood and watched the man walk ahead, the last of his obvious assets now on display. Finally, after much admiration, John muttered in firm appreciation, "What a smart ass."

* * *

In wracking waves of chill blades and sharp shivers, Aaron's body began to surrender to shock. John had to get him warm. What clothes were strewn outside would do little to battle a dangerous chill. John had little choice but to chance a run inside.

Packing the strips of T-shirt as tightly as he could into the chest wound, he could only offer a warm, lingering kiss to his lover's brow. As he let go, he murmured angrily in the fallen man's ear, "Don't you fucking leave me alone, Aaron."

In a rush of stumbling steps, he barreled into the side door of his house.

The slick, tiled floor of the sunroom nearly sent John headfirst into the breakfast table. He caught himself on the back of one of its chairs, accelerating off the teetering obstruction into the den.

Grabbing an old quilt off the couch and two flannel blankets off the recliners, John turned to head back out the door when Aaron's leather jacket caught his eye. The old thing was hanging on a hook on the closet door, having spent the last winter and summer cluttering up his house.

John grabbed the jacket and tore back out the door.

Aaron hadn't moved, but his shivers had intensified into full body spasms that caused him to gasp in tiny wisps of pain.

Only then did John let his first tear fall.

* * *

An uneventful ten minutes later the mission was complete: a wad of paper towels now sat on Aaron's lap and nary a doctor had to be lobbed in defense. John, eternally grateful that his old sweater hung low enough to hide any obvious signs of penile over-enthusiasm, sat back down in his recently abandoned lawn chair and watched the goings-on from the cooler-turned-pilot's seat.

"Damn! Knew I shouldn't have worn this," Aaron muttered as he furiously dabbed at the spilled beer on the leather aviator jacket he was still sporting. His tongue peeked out the left corner of his lips in stern concentration. "My mother's going to kill me."

John simply raised his eyebrow, banishing the *whippersnapper* from his oh-so tempted tongue.

Aaron rolled his eyes. "This was my father's jacket. She wanted to bury him in it, but…" He rolled his hand, allowing John's thoughts to lead him to the rightful conclusion.

"How old were you?"

"Twelve."

Remembering quite well the means and methods of a pre-teen riding high on a head of kamikaze-like steam, John guessed the *modus operandi*. "Tantrum or the silent treatment?"

Aaron shook his head, sheepishly. "Stole it from the church."

John knew he really shouldn't laugh, but oh, did he laugh.

Aaron snickered as he dipped his head boyishly. "If only my mother had your sense of humor, I would have seen the outside of my room in my teenage years."

John didn't believe for a moment that this man could be bowed by even the most adamant mother. "A regular hermit, I'm sure," he challenged with a gentle smile.

Lifting his head just in time to catch the soft upward turn of John's lips, Aaron said, "And you would know, Mr. Lone Man of the Driveway." John Castle actually felt himself blush. "So what's the story here, anyway?" Aaron went on. "You hiding from the law? The ex-wife?"

John lied quite effectively. "Like I said, just visiting some family friends, that's all."

Leaning back a bit from his perch on the cooler, Aaron made a grand sweep of the surrounding area with an exaggerated eagle-like glare. Finally, he shook his head. "Hate to tell you this, John, but there's not a family friend in sight."

John didn't miss a beat. "And that's why the doctor is smiling." Taking another swig from his much-nursed second beer, he decided to delve into some nosiness of his own. "Don't see any of your significant others around."

"Because you're looking at reconnaissance, my man" Aaron cheekily preened, then said, "Finding a place to land a '67 Airstream is no easy feat in this town."

"Ahh! So I'm your mark."

"More like my hidey-hole," Aaron quite easily confessed. "Sharing a cockpit with Beck is one thing, cozying up to him in an RV that smells like fish is another."

John chuckled. "So you bailed?"

"Didn't even bother with the 'chute." Aaron shrugged as he gave up on his jacket and pulled it slowly off of his broad shoulders. The play of finely sculpted muscles up and down his now mostly bare arms distracted John for a long, deliciously pleasurable moment, but he quickly latched back on to the conversation as Aaron explained, "I'm supposed to call them if I get any leads where they can park the Bass Mobile."

"They?" John hoped to God that his voice hadn't squeaked.

Nothing seemed amiss, however. "Beckett, Rosalyn, Annie, and Roach. And, no, you don't want to know why his Mama named him that."

"Fellow soldiers?"

Aaron nodded. "And a wife."

Damn. And double damn.

"Not mine," Aaron added, rather unnecessarily, as he took a more careful, contemplative sip of his beer. "Can't say I blame Roach for taking the leap, though. Annie's a hell of a woman."

One down. One to go. "And the fair Rosalyn?"

"She'd gut you with her pinkie for that one." Aaron unfolded a secretive smile. "She's the hardest-nosed soldier I know, a real bitch most of the time, but throw a football at her and she turns all giggly and soft." He shook his head fondly. "One hell of an odd girl."

Throwing all caution to the wind and effectively allowing his dick to drag him around, John leaned forward in his chair and asked with undeniably wicked interest, "And what's your story?"

Aaron leaned forward himself and narrowed his eyes into a sultry gleam. "Do you mean, what makes me all giggly and soft?"

To his eternal horror, John disintegrated into a pile of see-sawing mush. "No...yes...hell, I don't know."

"I doubt that," the pilot challenged.

"So do I."

The new but familiar voice fell down upon the pair like a gavel.

A young spindly man in his early twenties stood transfixed with his hands in his pants pockets. Short brown hair was tucked neatly inside a snug knit cap. It was black and it matched his turtleneck sweater. His pants were khaki-colored and loosely hugged his thin hips. He was reasonably tall, perhaps six feet, but there was no girth to his slim figure. His face was boyishly handsome, the kind fashion houses chose to sport their fall lines. Ebony leather loafers completed the tightly styled look.

Nearly leaping out of his skin, John gathered up what was left of his breath and glared up at the newly arrived, now-smirking man, "Shit, Liam! Make some noise next time."

"I made noise this time." At John's skeptical look, Liam glanced over at Aaron and asked, "Didn't I?"

Never taking his eyes off John, Aaron grinned sheepishly, then nodded. "He did."

When it became obvious that Aaron had seen Liam walking up all along, John seethed. "Why the hell didn't you say something?"

Aaron shrugged, all sugar-coated innocence. "Had other things on my mind. Besides, I figured he was one of those infamous distant family friends of yours." Aaron's eyes turned up to Liam, an unspoken question asking all.

Liam laughed a little louder than he should have. "That's one way to put it."

"Oh, for fuck's sake!" John growled under his breath as he shot up out of the lawn chair. "I was talking about your family, idiot! Not you."

"Good to know." A smile grew gently across Liam's lips, his softened gaze sweeping back down to Aaron. "I'm Liam Tasker, by the way."

"Aaron Chambers." He stood up from the cooler and offered his hand. "Nice to meet you, Liam."

Liam took the offering graciously enough, but turned his keen stare quickly back to John. "You never told me you knew someone in Auburn."

"I didn't! I don't!" Frustrated beyond the point of reason, John stormed up into Liam's face to warn, "And if you're wanting to keep *this* low key, you'd better back down right now, or this whole fucking town will know."

"Know what?" A girl's voice surprised them all.

John staved off a coronary. "Damn! Is your whole family part cat?"

"Only the best parts." A girl warring with her pre-teen years grinned up at John. She would one day be a beauty, all blond hair and gently filled curves, but the year of 12 had cursed her with blotched skin, bony hips, and legs too long for her body. The braces she wore on her teeth gently glinted in the mid-afternoon sun.

"Licia, shut up," Liam hissed at his sister.

"Ooh, are you two going to fight?" She literally bounced on the balls of her sneaker-clad feet, the child clearly beating out the soon-to-be burgeoning woman. "Is it about a girl?" Licia dragged out the last as only a little sister could.

"No!" both men shouted. Then John asked the siblings, "Where the hell is your father?"

Liam took a deep, cleansing breath and looked around. An amused twinkle settled in his right eye as he pointed out, "It seems he's not the only one missing."

John didn't even bother to look. He knew Aaron Chambers was gone.

* * *

Dwight Tasker had shown up exactly ten minutes too late to do John a scrap of good. The old man, loaded down with the whiskey John was now gulping at a disturbing rate, had meandered out of the odd little house with nary a sense of hurry or alarm. Despite the blue streak of highly creative profanity the two supposed friends were spewing at each other, Dwight didn't bother to rush. The same inattention went for his daughter, who sat cross-legged on the cooler taking prolific notes on swear words and body parts. Old Dwight just meandered out to the scene of the piteously covered-up lovers' spat, plopped himself down in the lawn chair and popped a couple of pork skins into his mouth.

It was this loud chewing of processed fat that brought a sudden quiet to the warfront.

Liam, all sweaty but still dapper, was the first to volley a round into the crunching audience. "Dad?"

Wiping an impressive abstract of grease onto his shirt sleeve, Dwight replied ever so calmly, "Yes, son? What is it?"

Stupefied to the point of mute awe, John could only watch as father and son ventured forth into the land of the ridiculous.

"Watchya doin'?" The fact that Liam's voice had now adopted a singsong quality was really the last of John's worries.

"I'm just eating my chips, son," Dwight enunciated without a hint of a twang or an uncalled for contraction. "What are you doing?"

"Liam's cussing out his boyfriend, Dad," Licia answered quite happily.

Liam dissolved into a guppy, all open mouth gulping and all.

"You really shouldn't do that, son."

"Shouldn't do…shouldn't do what?" Liam stuttered out.

John found his voice. "Do you really want the man to go into details, Liam?"

Dwight chuckled as he sucked down another pork skin. "Curse is what I meant you shouldn't do. Your mama raised you better than that."

"She did?"

John cringed, doubting Liam meant for that to be a question.

"Yes, you know she did. Now, this other *stuff* I don't have much to say about, except that you really shouldn't judge a family by its twang. Really, son, I raised you better than that." Dwight Tasker then let out a most tremendous burp.

From that point on, all logic was abandoned and all liquor heavily imbibed.

As the afternoon dragged on at a terrific crawl, it turned out that Dwight was really okay with his son's sexual orientation, and yes, not only had Dwight used those words, Licia had spelled them with aplomb. In fact, Dwight had suspected from the moment he met John that something more than buddy-talk was going on between the doctor and his son. As Dwight, in his most inebriated state, so elegantly put it, "What fool wouldn't go for a doctor who could fill a pair of jeans so well?"

John excused himself after that.

Liam and John still hadn't had a chance to work things out since their oh-so-colorful and very adult exchange. Not really relishing the thought of explaining to Liam what the hell he had been doing with Aaron, John took the opportunity to flee the scene. Out into the streets of Tiger Town he delved. And, no, he was most emphatically not looking for a certain pilot with great pecs and hard nipples he could nibble on for hours like candy. Nope, John Castle was not looking for Aaron Chambers. No way.

Now, if he stumbled upon a giant grey beast with "Make Love, Not War" mud flaps and happened to smell like tuna, well, that wasn't his fault. The Fates just had it in for the poor doctor.

After an hour of swimming through the maelstrom of Game Day maniacs, John was forced to come to the conclusion that the Fates were bitches and he a most miserable S.O.B.

Tail between his legs, he dragged his sorry ass back to the odd little house behind the iron gate.

* * *

Meanwhile, sweat-soaked, bare-chested Aaron Chambers tackled a man named Roach hard into the ground.

Roach did not take this lightly. Plucking the smaller man off of him, the six-foot-six M.P. tossed the scrap of measly pilot into a pile of leaves. Towering above him, Roach announced, "Enough of this shit. I'm going inside and fucking my wife until her tits fly off. Chambers, get your shit together."

As a somewhat dazed Aaron watched Roach march away to do his husbandly duties, he couldn't help but wonder, "What the fuck was going on?" He thought back on his other supposed compatriot. Beckett, a tower of a man himself, had also quickly tired of Aaron's "so-called shenanigans," as the Irish man so lyrically christened them.

Honestly, Aaron didn't know what either man was talking about. After settling the Big Fish in for a spell, the men had quickly dispersed into the chaos of the crowd to find a game of touch football. The fact that the *touch* turned inexplicably to *tackle* when Aaron was on the field went unnoticed until Beckett was untangling himself from a particularly aggressive pilot.

"What's the matter with you?" Beckett shoved the offending body off of his own. "You looking to get yourself killed?"

"No." Out of breath and holding his side, Aaron stumbled to his feet. "Just letting off some steam, man."

"Well, *man*, dial it down before you get yourself

hurt." Beckett patted him on the shoulder a little harder than necessary, and headed off in search of the famous "beer dog" of local lore.

Aaron wished him well on his mission and went right back to pile-driving the shit out of any fool unlucky enough to be caught.

It was less than an hour later when even Roach gave up.

He flopped back onto his appointed leaf pile and ran over the day in his head. Funny thing was that his mind kept tripping over a certain memory he quickly dubbed, "Damned John."

Well, not only was that totally unacceptable, it was stupid.

So, hauling himself out of the mountain of dead, crinkly color, Aaron grabbed his abandoned Air Force T-shirt and stomped off into a bevy of appreciative ladies. He'd show his dick who was boss.

* * *

The good thing about coming home with your tail firmly tucked between your legs is that an attentive lover notices and does his level-headed best to raise your sagging spirits. Liam, despite his faults, was an excellent rabble rouser. And after a heated, yet very succinct discussion on John making "let me fuck you" eyes at an impressively packaged stranger, Liam got down to his rabble-rousing business.

Which was exactly where a hot and bothered Aaron found them.

Much to Aaron's utter consternation, even after an hour of mutual attentiveness Aaron and his new female playmates hadn't graduated from *touch* to *tackle* sports. Sure, there were extenuating factors. The lovely ladies had been more than a bit tipsy, which only seemed to ironically bolster their Bible-belt inhibitions. And at one crucial point they were interrupted by a marching band practicing their maneuvers. All in all, for a man of his creative prowess, it had been a doable situation—if only his cock hadn't gotten an attitude.

Where the ladies offered soft touches and sweet nothings in his ear, his dick refused them more than a polite twitch in response. The little shit down below was holding out for something rougher, some manhandling, as it were. Never before had it shown this interest. This unexpected curiosity on its part was damned suspicious. Aaron would have even called this sudden change in attitude mutinous if he wasn't sure he could have got his buddy back on board if he really wanted to.

The *want* was the problem. His heart just wasn't in the effort. He wasn't looking for a sit-down conversation with his privates; he just wanted some base action and in turn some base satisfaction. It had been simple, up until "Damned John."

He'd already run out on the ripening situation once. When Liam, the man who was so obviously John's lover, had shown up, Aaron was left with little doubt that John had been flirting with him. Knowing he was the object of John's attention wasn't what had spooked Aaron, though; it was his own dick's reaction that had gotten him concerned. Whatever the man named John Castle had going for him, it had convinced Aaron's body that it might like a taste.

What the fuck was that about?

Well, this time, Aaron was going to find out. No more sidestepping the situation when no one was looking. He was going to face this head on.

So he marched straight back into the odd little battlefield that was the Tasker property. He didn't have a clue as to what he was going to say to John. He'd just play it by ear, keep his dick in line and get to the bottom of this... this... thing.

Hopping over the locked iron gate, he headed right up the gravel driveway to the house, but familiar voices out back delayed his knock on the front door. He had seen no need to bother the whole family when the man he needed to talk to was just around the side of the house. So Aaron, fresh from a round of sexual frustration, walked around back.

The first eyeful of flesh was innocent—the rest were not.

The back room of the odd little house behind the iron gate was used as a makeshift greenhouse. What once had been a screened-in back porch had been enclosed in the '70s with windows in frames an iconic shade of avocado green. Pale mustard-colored walls were stacked with wooden shelves which themselves were lined with brashly hued ceramic pots. It was a feast of the rainbow, with Liam and John adding their own colorful interpretations of the theme.

Braced against a waist-high potting table, John Castle stood naked from the waist down. The dark gray denim of his jeans pooled on the floor, with only one pant leg now still properly around a booted ankle. Powerful calves held steady wide-apart knees. Muscular thighs quaked to hold hips and groin firm as

Liam Tasker voraciously sucked John's cock down his bulging throat.

Aaron's mouth went dry.

The short brown strands of Liam's hair jerked violently with each thrust and each hard-won swallow. Bobbing up and down with the steady, hammering motion of a diesel-powered piston pumping its shaft, Liam's head thudded against John's groin. Liam's nose, with its nostrils flaring as it sucked in air, was shoved again and again into the wiry nest of dark pubic curls. Eyes clinched shut, hands fisted at his sides, Liam squeezed every ounce of strength out of his neck, face, and throat muscles. He looked to be in delicious agony, while John dissolved in perfect ecstasy.

Beneath the zipper of his jeans, Aaron felt his own cock fill.

John still wore his cream-colored sweater; it clung to his chest now as he heaved and fought through the pleasure threatening to devour him. His hands clenched the edges of the table, his short fingernails digging into the wood. John's lips lay open, his tongue jutting out to lick the beads of sweat from his strained mouth. His green eyes were open wide to the sky beyond the odd little room.

Engorged and caged in un-giving denim, Aaron's dick twitched and flared as if on fire.

John roared in sudden orgasm.

Aaron filled his pants with burning seed.

One closed his eyes fully sated; the other closed his eyes, ashamed.

Liam watched both in growing anger.

Chapter Three

Leather

The game was over. The stadium was empty. The sour tang of warm beer and stale nachos was whisked silently away on Mother Nature's cleansing breath as she blew into Auburn, Alabama, a harsher wind. Banners that had proudly bedecked the stadium gates for the last week now danced in forgotten tatters before they, too, were swept away into the night. Soda cups and pompoms, napkins and hot dog wrappers all tangoed eerily across the deserted pavers. The parties to either celebrate or to drown one's sorrows had moved inside the campers that littered every available square inch of green, or out into hotel rooms just beyond the Auburn city lights. Drunken stragglers lingered here and there, but mostly they did not linger long, as even their clouded senses knew a storm was coming.

The clock high in Samford Hall had doled out its midnight call no more than a brief half hour ago. Aaron didn't know the time any more than the mascot eagle did as it slept in its grand, yet netted aviary. Up and down the tiny streets the pilot wandered, too sober to get good and lost, too confused to really care. Huddled against the North Wind's heightening roar in his father's soiled leather jacket, Aaron hugged his arms tight to his chest as he slowly moved through the stadium's shadow.

He hadn't skipped the game. He had gone and cheered and drank and ate with all his friends as though nothing absurd had happened. No one had even questioned his sudden change of pants. After the game, after all the clichéd hoorahs and liquor-sweetened laughs, Aaron had slipped away from the tuna fish can that was their smelly home away from home and disappeared into the storms brewing both inside and outside his head.

While nature's rising fury was a known madness to the child born under wild Western skies, the swirling thoughts and razor-sharp doubts within Aaron's soul were a new chaos in which the young man now found himself struggling. He had been aroused, significantly aroused, by a man sucking off another man. He had seen a lot in his years abroad, and at home for that matter, with the Air Force, but nothing had so keenly affected him as the sight of John Castle being swallowed whole. That's where the confusion came in. Had Aaron suddenly developed a cock-rising interest in graphic man-on-man action in general? Or was it John's particular dick causing all of Aaron's upheaval?

"Where the hell did you go?" Doctor Dick, in the guise of one John Castle, suddenly popped up out of nowhere and strolled casually across the street to Aaron's side.

"Huh?" It wasn't the most intelligent response,

but it was all Aaron could grind out of the already overworked cogs churning in his head.

John scrunched down from his extra inch of height to give his face a proper look-see. "You look like shit."

"Thank you, John." The sarcastic answer came without a shred of thought on Aaron's part as he blinked at the doctor, still trying to catch up with the fact that John was actually there having this inane discussion with him. "You look like shit, too, by the way," Aaron thought it only polite to add.

John scowled in a threatening manner, but at this point Aaron simply didn't give a damn. He walked right past him before John could open his scowl in response.

A hand locked on to Aaron's bicep and attempted to spin him back around.

It didn't work.

Yanking his arm out of John's grasp, Aaron warned the doctor in one sentence, "You touching me right now would not be a good idea."

"What the fuck is wrong with you?" John snarled, but kept his hands to himself. "You disappear without a word and now you show back up acting like a first-class bastard."

Aaron dropped his shoulders at that. Okay, he was being a jerk, but that didn't mean he wanted to be called on it by another jerk. "Can we just drop this?" Aaron asked in place of an apology that he simply didn't have the fortitude to scrounge up in his current state of bastard-hood.

After an ugly moment of silence, in which Aaron cursed again this never-ending day, John surprised him by letting out a deep breath and saying in a reasonable and tired voice, "Yeah, okay."

Now Aaron did spin around. "What is with you, man?"

"Me?" The anger along with a fair share of stupefaction was back.

"Hot, cold, hot, cold." Aaron singsonged, trying to get a rise.

"And what about you?" John scoffed as he too broke out into taunting song, "Here, gone, here, gone."

"I've known you all of, what, half-an-hour? How the hell can there be that many "here, gone, here, gones"!" An amused twitch to John's lips which sent Aaron over the edge. "Get a life, Doctor whatever the shit your name is, and get the fuck out of mine!" With all the pent-up anger of the last hours, Aaron shoved John in the chest, sending the man stumbling awkwardly away from him.

John caught himself right before he went sprawling on to the cement. Still bent down, one hand on the ground, one knee bent below him, he stared coolly at Aaron and warned in an even voice, "You won't do that again."

The chills that went down Aaron's spine were not altogether unpleasant ones, but he brushed that quandary away for another time long down the line. Instead, he twisted his mouth into the most annoying smirk he could manage and countered just as coolly, "Won't be a problem, John. Never plan to touch your sorry ass again."

Bringing himself back up to full height, John smiled a long, cold smile. "Want to bet, flyboy?"

He tried to hold it in. He really did. Sometimes,

though, the raw emotion at a moment like this, even for a thoroughly disciplined soldier like himself, was just too much to beat back with cold, hard sense. So Aaron finally just let it all go—and broke out into a feverish episode of raucous laughter.

"The first time," he struggled out between bouts of jovial hiccupping, "I let that pass... but the second 'flyboy'... it's just too much, doc." He bent over at the waist, bellowing in all-consuming laughter.

A smile curled reluctantly across John's lips as the green darkened a shade in his eyes. "I'm thinking I could hate you, Aaron whatever-the-shit your name is."

Aaron broke out into a grin that could light a night sky as he dared, "Bring it on."

In a bolt of lightning and a frightful twisting of wind, Mother Nature did just that.

Rain slammed down on them with the ferocity and recklessness of a breached dam. Within a startled heartbeat, the pellets of ice cold water drowned the two men in its chill.

Aaron looked dumbly up at the suddenly warring sky. "What the hell..."

"We need to move!" John yelled above the deafening torrent. "Now!"

Aaron didn't question further, he just moved. The sheets of pouring rain made the men move slowly. Arms held over their faces, an ever-growing, howling wind battering them John and Aaron had barely made it across the street when a siren's wail suddenly ripped through the air.

"Tornado!" Aaron yelled as he grabbed John's arm and hauled ass into a ditch. Barely three feet deep, the culvert sat lopsidedly, snuggled up to the old street's curbless cement. Water already lay at its bottom, the sudden downpour quickly leaving its mark.

Aaron hadn't even realized where they were until, lying on his belly, he squinted his eyes up to see the Taskers' monstrous elm tree. As the water in the tiny roadside ditch started to rise at an alarming rate, Aaron cursed above the fury of the storm. "Fuck! We're either going to drown or be taken out by that damn elm."

"Just hold your breath… and don't make the tree angry."

Aaron dropped his head to his arms and laughed.

The rain turned to hail. Tiny rocks with razor-sharp edges pummeled the backs of the men as they lay hunkered in the swelling waters of the ditch.

Aaron's hands were slowly cut to shreds as they covered the back of his bowed head. "Ow."

As he carefully rearranged himself so that the rising water was still a safe distance from his hidden face, John said over the wind, "Suck it up, soldier."

"Yeah, that helps." Aaron rolled his eyes despite them being tightly shut. "Antagonize your ditch-mate before he has to save your sorry ass."

"Shut up and cower."

Mother Nature turned bitch. In a roar of fantastic horror, she gathered all of her flailing winds together and ruthlessly spun them. The sky itself creaked amidst the crippling pressure of the newly born tornado. The winds turned to knives as they screwed the electrified clouds into the ground.

Despite John's notorious hard-assed façade, he simply shook in terror.

A bloodied hand reached out from the storm and,

finding the back of the doctor's neck, squeezed reassuringly.

The long spindly fingers of the elm's broad branches began to shiver. Like feathers plucked from a dead chicken, the autumn-kissed leaves one by one were torn from their roots and summarily sucked up into the hellish sky.

The sound was tremendous as the mouth of the storm moved directly overhead of the old tree. Stripped bare of its leaves, the elm—now skeleton— succumbed to its fate.

In a horrific final roar, the tree was ripped from the ground and twisted terribly into the sky. Mother Nature cackled in the guise of thunder as she tossed the ravaged elm directly down—right through the Tasker house.

Neither man bore witness to the joined fates of old tree and home, for both men were now under water, holding their breaths and praying for the end to mercifully come.

* * *

John was the first to break free from their would-be watery grave. He bolted out of the muddied water breathless and pale. Frantically, he gulped in the now-still air, filling his lungs as fast as he dared. Once some sort of equilibrium had been reached in his oxygen-starved mind, he realized he stood in the water alone.

"Aaron!" he yelled as he thrashed about the mud around him, the moonless night as much as the downed power lines blinding him from seeing anything but shadows. He called out again, "Aaron!"

"Right… right here," Aaron's voice gurgled over John's shoulder.

Spinning around as fast as the muck he was mired in allowed, John found standing there a pitiful version of a drowned rat wearing a very familiar aviator's jacket. "You're alive!"

"Sure about that, are ya?" Still spluttering out water between deep, self-assuring breaths, Aaron glared up at John.

Grabbing Aaron's face between his muddy hands, he planted a kiss on the man's forehead. "Hell, yeah, I'm sure."

Aaron's hands grabbed John's wrist in a knee-jerk reaction. He froze when he didn't know whether he was about to push John away or draw his touch closer. Either way, he figured he was screwed. So, shaking his head, he took a soggy step back and immediately missed the warmth of John's skin on his cheeks. He finally managed a weak grin as he admitted, "Good to see you, too, doc."

Even from feet away and swallowed in the never-changing dark, John scrutinized him with the practiced eye of a physician. Once all limbs had been satisfactorily, although muddily, accounted for, John asked, "You all right?"

"No." That was simple.

"Good." John snorted, looking down at his equally disastrous self. "Neither am I."

Aaron seemed to lean closer to John for a moment, doing a cursory survey, John guessed. Apparently he passed muster. Aaron pulled himself back and gave a betrayed look to the sky. "I don't care what all you good folks say…it sure as hell didn't sound like a train."

John snickered in spite of himself.

"John…"

The change in his voice quickly broke John's momentary revelry. "What?" he asked slowly.

"Look." Aaron raised his arm with a tremble and pointed behind John.

When he whipped around to see, his very breath deserted him in a choked, "Fuck."

Then, without another word, the men simply ran.

* * *

The odd little house was no more. The elm tree had crushed it beneath its twisted carnage. The end frames of the old farmhouse still stood but at wrong angles. Leaning inward toward the tree that had essentially torn the home apart, the wooden beams formed a skeletal canopy over the still-settling ruins. There was little more remaining upright, most of the weathered structure having crumbled into a thousand ill-shaped splinters.

"Are they here?" A breathless Aaron pulled up beside him.

John didn't so much as blink.

Aaron yanked hard at John's arm. "God damn it, John! Are the Taskers here?"

Snapped out of it, John still didn't answer, just running instead to the parking shed on the far side of the property. He nearly collapsed in relief when he found the building blessedly empty.

Aaron caught up with him. "They're gone?"

"Yeah." John ran his trembling hand through his hair. "They must be." Although he had no idea where they had gone. Liam, he could easily imagine storming off into the night once he found John gone. His truck missing was definitely a relief, if not a surprise. John honestly had no idea where Dwight would have gone in the middle of the night. But Dwight's old sedan was nowhere on the property, and Licia, despite her precociousness, sure as hell couldn't drive, so…

A nagging pit of dread grew in John's gut. "Licia!"

"She's here?" Aaron asked, wide-eyed.

"I don't know," John said as he cast another horrified glance at the remains of the Tasker house. "Damn it! I don't know."

"Come on!" Aaron commanded as both men tore off toward the home.

The house was virtually destroyed. With every step they took, hope of finding anything salvageable or any corner survivable dwindled. As John and Aaron circled the debris field, they were shocked to find the back room more or less still standing. Its framed windows were all broken, glass strewn everywhere, but the old back porch miraculously retained most of its shape. A V-shaped crook formed by the main trunk of the elm and one of its higher branches had effectively straddled the makeshift greenhouse, maiming but not outright destroying the 1970s quaint relic.

"Do you see that?" Aaron asked. "There's no way that should have—"

"I know," John answered in growing awe. "It shouldn't."

Optimism suddenly smoldered again in Aaron's brown eyes. He slapped John's shoulder as he encouraged, "Let's move."

They ran to the lone remaining door of the structure,

the back room's avocado green door that lay broken off of its hinges. The bottom half of the wooden door still remained wedged into the widely distorted frame, hampering easy entrance into the ruins of the house. Aaron hardly slowed down at all as he hurriedly climbed up and through the blocked doorway.

With a little less grace but just as much urgency, John quickly followed on his heels. His work boots slid on the rain-slicked cement floor, barely catching himself before he plowed into Aaron.

Aaron was stopped dead still. Determination and a flickering of anguish warred for control of his face as he stared at their path. "Nobody could have survived in there." The interior doorway that had once led to the kitchen now opened onto a minefield of jagged glass, dagger-like shards of appliance metal and stripped electrical lines snapping and sparking in the ruthless night.

Undaunted, John bolted right past Aaron. "Then I'll drag a dead body out of here, but I'm not leaving until I know for sure." Grabbing a downed bookshelf, he yanked it out of their path, letting it and its remaining ceramic pots crash loudly to the floor.

Quickly brushing away the debris cloud that had enveloped him thanks to John's good-hearted but reckless machinations, Aaron grabbed John by his shoulder and pulled him back. "If only the cell towers weren't down, this would be a hell of a lot easier." Once Aaron had seen the destruction the storm had wrought on the possibly occupied house, he had of course tried his cell phone. The previously strong signal had disappeared completely.

"Yeah, I know." Yielding to the probable disaster

training of a soldier, John brushed that freaking lock of hair off of his forehead. "But we're more than capable of doing this the old-fashioned way."

Aaron absolutely agreed. "So stop talking and start digging."

* * *

As the minutes of cold, backbreaking work passed, both men were silent. While John used his extra height to reach the taller of the obstructions, Aaron worked ceaselessly on his knees. Progress was slow, if existent at all.

"Fuck," Aaron gritted out as he rose up and looked John straight in the eye. "There's blood here. A lot of it."

"Let me see," John demanded, nudging Aaron unapologetically out of his way. He had thought the blood would tell him something, anything, to help them find Licia, but the frighteningly large splatter of fresh blood told him nothing except that they had to hurry. Standing up, John yelled into the night, "Licia! Can you hear me?" The shout wasn't new but its underlying desperation was, and it sickened him to hear it in his own voice. "Licia!"

"Shut up and help me." Aaron yanked John back down to the ground, where he was still studying the blood pattern. "We find a trail and we'll find her."

It was simple logic, but to a panic-stricken John, it was sheer brilliance. "Let's do it!"

Like anything that happened in this town, it was easier said than done. There was no light except the pinprick of illumination Aaron's keychain flashlight afforded, and moving one piece of debris, however slightly, sent another ten pieces falling on top of the searching men. It was an arduous span of long, hard minutes but finally, a thin line of still-wet blood was uncovered under a row of roofing shingles. Unfortunately the trail led to a dead end.

"Where the hell is she?" John asked.

"Maybe she got out?" Aaron suggested.

"Or she's under there." John stared at the blood trail's dead end: a mangled pile of sheetrock, metal shielding and large kitchen appliances. A mouse couldn't have squeezed itself safely under the tortured mass. "If she is…" But he absolutely refused to finish the thought.

Aaron did. "Then she'll be damn glad that we're about to get her out."

"Yeah." John sighed.

"You mean, 'Hell, yeah.'"

John never got the chance to reply as the world once again broke around them.

It sounded like the very bones of the earth had suddenly been snapped in two. A catastrophic *Crack!* followed by a horrendous fingernails-on-chalkboard whine sent both men to the floor.

The murdered elm was moving.

The long-abandoned fruit cellar beneath the broken house had finally buckled under the tremendous weight of the tree. The load-supporting beams of the cellar cracked like twigs, bending the braces of the house's foundation until they whined in fatal complaint. The floor beneath John and Aaron's bodies actually shivered for long, agonizing seconds before it completely crumbled to the cellar below.

The pilot and the doctor followed the house

unwillingly into the ground.

* * *

A frightening silence awaited Aaron as he slowly regained his senses. "John?" he squeaked out from under a pale yellow countertop and a toaster oven.

Some rustling around and a few grunts preceded John's wary but relatively healthy-sounding, "Aaron?"

Aaron wearily dropped his head to his arms. "Can I go home now?"

John's answering chuckle was suddenly replaced by a sickened gasp "Oh, God, I found her."

"Where?" Aaron scrambled toward John, sheetrock dust and hair-breadth splinters of wood haloing his every hurried move. He was coughing when he finally crawled to John's side. "Where is she?" he asked again, his heart skipping when he didn't see or hear any sign of Licia.

"She's here." John was kneeling over, his hand clutching at something beneath the crushed refrigerator.

As Aaron shone the penlight into the mangled appliance's shadows, a pale hand of little girl fingers came frighteningly into view. Only a wrist and a short stretch of forearm could also be seen as the rest of her arm disappeared back beneath the refrigerator's bulk. Her hand apparently was the only part of her body to have escaped the crushing weight. "Is she alive?" Aaron choked out as he simply stared at the scene straight out of a macabre film.

"Yeah." John wasn't calling out to her, wasn't doing anything to help her. He simply held her wrist under his middle finger, feeling her pulse.

Aaron feared John was drifting into shock. Unfortunately neither of them had the time for that. He reached down and slapped John hard upside the back of his head. "Get your shit together, Doctor!"

John didn't say anything—which said a lot. After only seconds, his so-called shit was once again gathered together, and he was able to turn his attention back to where it belonged. He lay his head down to the floor and called out gently, "Licia? Can you hear me? It's John."

The men froze and listened anxiously, but the silence remained hauntingly unbroken.

Deciding to take on the bad cop role to John's good cop approach, Aaron barked out in his best military voice, "Licia! You need to answer us. Now."

The silence continued to hang in the cellar's air untouched.

Aaron gulped back the raw edges of his worry, filling the void with a needless, "We have to get her out of there."

"We move anything, we might make it worse." John took a deep, shuddering breath. "She's weak."

"Then we've got to move now. I can lift the refrigerator up a little and you can pull her out."

John shook his head, his fingers never leaving the tiny arm. "You've got to go for help. Moving the weight pinning her arm down might only exacerbate her injury. If she started to bleed heavily…The two of us alone can't save her, Aaron. I can't risk her bleeding out when she's relatively stable right now."

"But…"

"Now!" John growled, then softened his tone.

"Just go. I'll stay here."

Aaron blew out a frustrated breath, then said, "All three of us may be staying here. Look around, John."

Instead, John squeezed his eyes shut. "Damn it, I know." He paused. "Never say die, Aaron," he whispered.

Aaron smiled softly at the chosen mantra. "Okay," he whispered in return. Then, running a hand over his face, Aaron scanned the debris, trying to find a place to start.

"I'll help." John moved to let go of Licia's wrist.

"No," Aaron quickly vetoed. "You keep right on holding that girl's hand. She needs to know she's not alone anymore." Giving up on finding the right place to start digging, Aaron just dove in to the nearest pile of debris.

After only a few minutes of the hard labor, Aaron realized just how long this was going to take. "So talk, Doctor. Show me some of that bedside manner you M.D.s are famous for."

John didn't skip a beat in replying, "You know I'm fucking Liam."

Aaron almost fell right on his ass. He threw a look of incredulity over at John, not giving a damn if the bastard could actually see him or not. "Well, yes, John. I dare say now we all know that."

John nodded toward Licia. "She knows, Aaron."

"That's the point, Sherlock." Aaron chucked a can of lima beans against the makeshift wall.

John felt like chocking a certain pilot. "Idiot, she knew before."

There was a distinct lack of noise from the other side of the cellar. John thought maybe Aaron had fallen into the toaster oven before Aaron called, sounding dumbstruck, "But I thought..."

The dumbstruck part, John totally got. "Yeah, so did I, but I..." He stopped to correctly spread blame. "Well, Liam and I were both wrong."

"Ahh." More silence before the tossing of debris recommenced. "And the old man?" he asked ever so casually.

John winced. "Knew."

"And?" Aaron drew out the word in almost comic nosiness.

"Better with it than we are." John sighed, still infinitely confused at that realization.

"Interesting."

John sighed. "To put it mildly." Damn, now came the newest crux of John's ever-expanding dilemma. "So, you knew, too?" he asked.

"Yeah," Aaron replied in a suspiciously low-key manner, but before John had the time to ask how, Aaron quickly shuffled the conversation. "So, John, you got a life story?"

John snorted.

"Okay, dumb question," Aaron admitted with an impressive lack of embarrassment.

"Yes, it was." John felt it necessary to confirm.

"Smart ass," Aaron rejoined. "And for being such an annoying shit, you lose your life story privileges." He took great care in clearing his throat before beginning dramatically, "I was born in a small town..."

The laugh just burst from John's mouth. "You mean a small town like, oh, I don't know, say, Los Angeles? Seattle? Phoenix?" Aaron simply didn't exude the small-town charm with which John was extremely familiar.

"Colorado," Aaron replied simply.

"Ahh!" John nodded his head, knowing all along he had been right. "Denver."

"Ahh! Limon!" Aaron eagerly mocked. "East of Denver, out on the plains." His voice turned pleasantly wistful. "Home to 2,000 good people, and the keeper of endless blue skies."

A soft smile ever so gently kissed John's lips. One of Aaron's lovers was clearly the sky. "So, the pilot thing was egged on by…"

"My father's Air Force ribbons."

With an embarrassed cough that he quickly disguised as a clever clearing of his throat, John confessed with barely a wince, "Jacksonville, Florida."

There was another of those unnerving silences. John would really have preferred another chucked can of beans. Finally, Aaron managed to churn out, "You're kidding."

John knew the torment wasn't over so he just kept his mouth shut.

"You?" Aaron actually chortled. "The Whippersnapper Man?"

John rolled his eyes and bit his very tempted tongue.

Aaron was doing more of that snorting/yodeling thing that really was cute if quite a bit annoying. John could handle that. What he couldn't handle however was Aaron's accusation. "A big-city boy?" Aaron chirped.

"*Boy*?" John squeaked out in unintentional high-pitched objection. He tried it again, only deeper,

"Don't you mean *man*?"

"Maybe," Aaron too quickly allowed, as John could feel the bastard smirking from across the room. "I don't know, though," Aaron irritatingly taunted. "I guess I'll have to ask Liam about the boy thing." He snickered.

John did not.

After a few minutes of quiet toil, Aaron ventured again, "And your impending doctor-hood, what brought that on?"

John answered easily, "Money." It might be ugly, but it was the simple truth.

"The American dream," Aaron cracked.

"Wise guy," a girl's voice weakly choked out.

"Licia?" Startled, John quickly dropped his head back down to the floor and peered into the darkness under the refrigerator. His grasp on the tiny arm remained tight. "You can hear me?"

"Duh."

"I like this girl," Aaron said.

Royally waving his hand for the menial work to continue, John snapped at Aaron, "Do I see daylight?"

"God, I hope not. If we've been here that long…" Aaron could feel the moss-green daggers being thrown his way. Turning back to his slowly diminishing pile of rubble, Aaron muttered brightly, "But I get your point. Dig."

Only seconds passed before Licia's fragile voice brought the true situation into ugly light. "I hurt."

John put on his best doctor voice and asked with as much professional detachment as he could muster, "Where exactly do you hurt, Licia?"

"My arm," she answered immediately.

"Yeah, I bet," John tried his best not to sound relieved. There were so many other things that could be going wrong in her crushed body, her arm alone hurting was an ironic relief. "But I don't want you to try to move it, okay? Hold real still."

"Okay."

"You hurt anywhere else?" the doctor in him had to ask for clarification's sake.

"No," she replied with little hesitation. "But this fucking refrigerator's heavy and I'm scared shitless."

"Licia!" John snapped.

Across the room, Aaron simply laughed. "If there ever was a time for her to cuss, John, I'd say it was now." Aaron grunted as he tossed another chunk of house to the side. "You know, Licia, I think I might even join you." He revved up his voice and shouted, "Shit! Fuck! And damn, damn, damn!"

"You're not helping," John deadpanned as the girl giggled.

Aaron figured it was a good time to point out again, "But I am the one digging here, John, so…"

"Shut the fuck up?" Licia helpfully filled in the blank.

John threw out the only real threat he could think of. "I'm talking to your brother."

"Bully," Licia predictably fussed.

"Yeah, big, bad bully," Aaron brightly backed her up as another kitchen cabinet was tossed rebelliously to the wayside.

Rolling his eyes, John begged, "Where the hell is your father?"

"I don't know." The little girl still within Licia Tasker then peeked out of her voice to admit, "I can't feel my fingers."

"Aaron…" John began.

"I know," Aaron answered simply and worked a little faster.

"C-cold," she suddenly stammered.

A rustling of leather preceded Aaron's coat being tossed over to John. "Give her this."

He looked incredulously from the jacket to the refrigerator and simply asked, "How?"

"Lieutenant!" a woman's voice suddenly hollered down from above. "Lieutenant Chambers!"

"Sergeant?" Aaron called out, almost laughing, "I ever tell you that you're a godsend?"

The sergeant barked back, "No, sir! And I don't think this is the time, sir. We've got help coming, Lieutenant. Hold on."

Exhausted, Aaron dropped down to his knees and sighed, "Meet Rosalyn."

John's mind was whirring in utter relief, but he was able to remember a certain trait of the fair Rosalyn. "She giggles?"

There was no reply but a chuckle, as blessed activity began to buzz overhead. Still holding Licia's hand tight in his own, John let the relief flow through him. He dropped his gaze to his lap, where Aaron's jacket still lay. A mark on its leather caught his eye. Lifting it up into the narrow beam of newly revealed moonlight, John could see the mark was in fact a repair. John's breath caught in his throat as he recognized the telltale shape of a bullet wound.

* * *

The air lay stagnant, stinking of blood and John's

tears. Sweat bubbled up on John's skin in contrast to the chill bumps that covered Aaron's. Aaron had stopped trembling; the blankets and jacket having succeeded at least in that. The leather coat pillowed Aaron's head off of the pavers, the blood seeping onto it inconsequential to John. Later he'd get the thing cleaned. "I swear," he whispered.

Other than John's fervent though useless words, the silence lay on the horizon like a long-dead beast. Prod and poke as much as John liked, the monstrous silence would not depart. He had called 911 again. Promises were made once more that help was on its way, but John was beginning to fear that the whole world lied.

Even the weather was odd and deceiving. It was still yet muggy, a disturbing presence that brought both unease and simple comfort. It was like an old woman sitting by your side keeping you company while she picked your pockets clean.

John felt ill.

Turning to the side, he vomited up his warm beer. The acid taste lingered in his throat, tickling his gag reflex to hurl again and again.

Through all the gut-wrenching heaves, however, his hands not once left Aaron's body.

Between twisted breaths, John looked up and begged the moon for the night to be gone.

The vomiting lasted for a moment shy of eternity, or so John would have sworn. With his attention finally concentrated again fully on Aaron, he met with a modicum of success. Having stemmed the bleeding of his head wound, he was able to hold Aaron's hand. He squeezed his lover's fingers within his own, in desperate need of affirmation. But still, John shook in shameless terror.

He'd give his soul to feel those reassuring fingers from the height of the storm on his neck again.

So, John prayed.

And John's prayers were sent, but the heavens continued to look down upon him with no answers.

His eyes dropped sadly back down to his fallen "angel." The term brought a welcomed wisp of a smile to his beleaguered face. The tears had long since dried.

John tried to move, his muscles locking up and beginning to scream for attention, but his knees had finally gone numb beneath him.

"Why are we always on the ground?" John choked out. "You have wings, after all."

Minutes that lasted hours later, blessed sound finally filled the night sky.

With the sirens growing mercifully closer, John Castle removed the makeshift bandage from Aaron's chest. He hadn't remembered about the leather coat's frighteningly similar scar until tonight. Haunted, John traced the bullet's hole in his lover's skin.

Chapter Four

Chocolate

A morning after a disaster was a lot like a Salvador Dali dream. Clock faces melted down walls, their fanciful numbers slowly dripping away into anonymity. Long-legged nightmares walked right up to your face and frowned at your wandering eye. Blood-red roses hung in the air crying solitary painted-on tears. Reality had little to do with the world in those moments, as God twirled his moustache and grinned.

Folding his hands up under his chin, John Castle watched as another church group came bustling in to his suddenly surreal world. Wrapped all up in coats that oftentimes hid pajamas underneath, the good ladies and men of Columbus, Georgia, passed out bottled water and little boxes of whole-grain cereal. The already overcrowded emergency room swelled with their good-willing presence and John smiled gratefully as he was handed his third brightly colored box of the totally weird morning.

After being rescued by a handful of Air Force pilots and a gaggle of girls flaunting suspiciously intimate knowledge of Aaron, the medics had whisked Licia away. With the local hospital already overflowing with storm victims, the EMTs had decided to head straight to Columbus, a nice-sized town just over the state line. Thankfully, they had allowed John and Aaron to ride with them, otherwise the men would still be stuck in Auburn. All communication lines were down and the men wouldn't have had a hope in hell in finding their own way to Columbus. Rosalyn and the rest of Aaron's buddies had decided to stay and help with the search and rescue in the area, while keeping an eye out for any signs of Licia's family. John just hoped the rest of the Taskers had fared better than their youngest.

"Here you go." A white pharmacy bag filled with bandages, disinfectant, aspirin, and other first-aid favorites was plopped down on John's lap. Aaron, the bearer of the kit, towered above him wearing a put-upon scowl.

John sighed. "You know, I could have gone to get these."

"Yeah, and when somebody finally came out here and started spouting doctor-speak at me, what the hell was I supposed to do?"

"Listen." John stopped, thought about it a little, then added, "Maybe nod."

"Sure, I'd nod and then Licia's whisked off to some quack clinic in Saskatchewan."

"Quack clinic?" It was a new term for John. He let it play slowly off of his tongue.

"Sorry."

"Saskatchewan?" John just couldn't let that one go.

Aaron smiled wistfully. "Knew a girl once."

"I'm sure you did," John muttered pettily under his breath.

Thankfully, Aaron didn't hear a thing as he was still carrying on a mile a minute. Kneeling down at John's feet, in a position John simply refused to think about, Aaron was busy sorting through their collection of cereal. "So what did we get this time?" He looked at the newest arrived box and shook it. "Hope there's a toy."

"What are you, five?"

"Twenty-two." Aaron preened as only the truly young can.

"And they let you fly planes?"

A scrumptiously cocky grin played across his lips. "Want to see my wings?"

"Yes." The answer was out of his mouth before his brain had the chance to kick the shit out of his apparently ravenous penis.

Before Aaron could reply to this unplanned and stupidly risky volley, one of the larger of the bottle-carrying women ran into Aaron. He was still kneeling on the floor examining their granular stash when suddenly he flew one way and the woman toppled the other. Apologies were offered all around and John and Aaron both got another bottled water out of it. John was sure, however, that Aaron's tiny "Ow!" was supposed to go unnoticed.

It didn't. John sighed and held out his hands on his lap. "Let me see."

"Huh?" An imaginary dunce cap suddenly plopped down on Aaron's head.

John rolled his eyes at the dumb act. "I heard you. You 'ow'ed."

"Is that a word?"

Knowing where Aaron's only significant injuries were, John commanded, "Hands."

Aaron scoffed and didn't move an inch. "They're fine. I washed them."

"With water and everything!" John put on his rarely used "Now!" face.

"Shut up," Aaron grumbled and shoved his hands not too gently into John's lap. "Happy?"

With those hands so close to certain parts, John shifted to make sure Aaron didn't know just how happy he was. Grabbing the iodine from the little collection of goodies Aaron had just brought, John assured with a pleasant curl to his lips, "This is going to hurt."

"Bring it on," Aaron said.

John rolled his eyes. "Last time you said that we had a tornado fall on our heads."

Aaron quirked his brow in an unreadable expression as he softly repeated John's words from the night before. "Never say die, John."

* * *

"Never say die." The words fluttered off of Dr. John Castle's lips as lightly as a whispered prayer. The solemnity they deserved, he just couldn't find. His lover had that effect on things, on people—John guessed on the universe in general. Once anything, whether it be a set of carefully chosen words or a cynical soul, was touched by Aaron Chambers, it had no choice but to come away from the experience lighter and brighter.

John chuckled harshly to himself, "Yeah, he's just a shitload of sunshine."

"Excuse me, sir?" The hospital aide looked up

from her clipboard of paperwork. "Did you say something?"

"Doctor." He ignored her question as he fumbled with a string on the leg of his sweatpants. "I'm a doctor."

"I had no idea." She looked almost apologetic.

Twitching his shoulders upward was all John's exhausted body could manage for a shrug. "It doesn't matter."

"But I'm sure we can skip some of these forms if you're here on staff?" She looked up at him hopefully.

They both knew hospital regulations said no but neither seemed in the mood to care. John gave her a weak smile, "I'm on staff at Bay Medical. My…" He stopped and cursed the world. "My friend is stationed at Tyndall."

Giving his hand an awkward pat, she stood and said gently, "I'll see what I can do, sir… Doctor." The girl and her forms flitted away.

Her absence left him with a surprisingly sharp ache of emptiness. He was alone now in the waiting room. It was the first moment he had had to himself. No EMTs screaming over wailing sirens. No cops asking him dumb questions, telling him dumb things. No nurses, no aides, no… no… Aaron. John slammed his eyes shut, crumbling over his knees. The mere existence of those two words together anywhere in his mind was like a shiv to the gut.

"No Aaron," he forced the damning phrase from his chapped and suddenly trembling lips. "No Aaron… no Aaron…" he repeated the words again and again, "No Aaron… no Aaron." As the mantra spun quicker, more frantic, more sickening, the meaning of the words changed. John was begging now, begging his lover not to leave him, "No, Aaron! No… Don't go… God, don't go!"

* * *

"You folks need anything?" A beanpole of a nurse with dyed red hair bent down and nosed herself into John and Aaron's personal space. She didn't look at either one of the men, just John's in-progress handiwork. "A couple of those might need stitches."

John rolled his eyes. "No, they won't."

Before she could counter, Aaron chirped in cheerily, "He knows. He's a doctor."

"Oh." She pulled back, looking crestfallen.

Aaron took a real long look at her and couldn't help cringing in empathy at her youth. He quirked a lopsided grin at her as he confided, "But he's not a very good doctor. Best to check on me in a bit." He added a soft wink.

She gently smiled. "Yes, sir, I will." Aaron watched her walk away.

John suddenly dabbed one of Aaron's scratches with a little more gusto than was necessary. When Aaron turned his glare back to him, John icily informed him, "Thank you for that."

Aaron was genuinely surprised to find a shard or two of hurt swimming around those green eyes. He quickly laughed at it. "I think your ego can take it. Hers couldn't."

John shook his head. "Textbook hero complex."

Aaron just smiled. "Nope, I've just been in her shoes a couple of times." Shrugging his shoulders, he added in honesty, "You know, too young to be where you're at. Scared shitless you'll screw it up. Not a good place."

"Why did you leave yesterday?" John asked out of the clear blue.

Aaron winced. He had expected the question, of course, but not right now. He looked to his left, to his right, and finally straight ahead. He winced again. Not right now and certainly not *here*. *Here* being on his knees, in front of the problem, holding the problem's hand. "I…" he began, planning to say something wry or maybe just stupid to throw the doctor off course, but instead found himself babbling out hard honesty. "I don't know why I left. Just needed to."

"So, it wasn't because you knew that Liam and I…"

"Fucked?" Aaron helpfully completed the awkwardness.

John snorted, clearly not taking any offense at the crude categorization of the relationship. "Yeah."

"No," he answered, his gaze never wavering from John's eyes.

"Good." After long, comfortable moments, John finally broke eye contact and nodded his head once firmly. It was as if he was dismissing that part of the conversation, chucking the topic far away from the here and now. "All done," he declared as he looked down at Aaron's hands still gently held within his fingers. Both men watched as John's thumb unconsciously rubbed tiny circles of comfort into the heart of Aaron's offered palm. "Feel better?" he asked with a peculiar strain to his voice.

"Feel like I've been run over by a truck." And he

did. Aaron hurt all over and dreaded having to try to stand back up. Sure, the linoleum floor was hell on his knees, and he could really use a shower, and a chocolate bar sounded ungodly good right now, but— but the heat of those long, strong fingers on his skin...

He flubbed out the first thing that came to his suddenly overtaxed brain. "I think I may just have to sit here for a while and slip into a coma, or something equally refreshing." Aaron immediately felt like an idiot but an idiot that wasn't moving an inch.

"Yeah?" The sweet surprise in the doctor's voice brought Aaron's eyes back to up to John's face.

Cocking his head just a little to the side, Aaron confessed with an uncomfortable yet tingling lack of doubt, "Yeah."

"John!" Liam's voice called out a bit too close to be at first sight, but the man betrayed no other signs that he had been using his cat-like skills again.

"Johnny!" Dwight Tasker joined the hollering, his gaze never sparing Aaron a glance as he rushed toward them.

Aaron was off his knees and back up on his feet fast enough to look conspicuously guilty. A quick glance at Liam and his cold stare assured Aaron that the man hadn't missed the confessional move.

"Where is she?" a weary-looking Dwight was asking, as the older man anxiously brushed Aaron aside. "They said she was here."

From there the world dissolved into the much-feared doctor-speak as two M.D.s and a terrified father exchanged long words and longer explanations. Aaron gladly fell back into the white noise of the emergency room.

Unfortunately, some of the most infuriating noise came from his own head. John's touch he couldn't get out of his mind. The feel of the smooth, unblemished skin of such long, nimble fingers against his body had almost been too much to take. Aaron had used the pain of the scratches to center him back on a path he was more willing to take, a road of simple friendship and nothing more. It was a hell of a hard path to stay on when John Castle stood on the roadside.

But Aaron had no choice.

Did he?

No, he didn't. The admonition, the warning, the damned foolishness of the words "Don't ask. Don't tell," kept screaming at him. He clung to the words as he did the pain. His career was the very core of his soul, the foundation to every goal in his life. He wouldn't throw it all away on a foolish whim of his dick.

He wouldn't.

No way.

And the sight of John now comforting Liam with a kiss would not change that.

Nope, wouldn't change a fucking thing.

* * *

While he was busy relaying the little bit of knowledge he had about Licia's condition, John noticed Aaron strategically retreat. He didn't blame him. By the time he was done explaining what he did know and excusing what he didn't know, John was getting stinking tired of the sound of his own voice. Finally, he suggested Dwight might have better luck talking to the actual hospital staff himself. The older man hurried off, leaving Liam and his disappointed scowl behind.

"Where the hell did you go last night?" Liam said as he moved aggressively into John's personal space. "I woke up and you were gone. Did you even come to bed? Or was it somebody else's ass you crawled into?"

It was either kiss him or kill him. So John had kissed him to shut him up.

Pulling back from his lover of six months, John wasn't sure he'd made the right choice.

"What was that for?" Apparently John wasn't the only one catching the weird vibes emanating between them. Liam absently touched his barely reddened lips as he waited for an answer.

"I'm glad you're okay." John tried to flash a smile, but immediately knew it didn't work. Unlike his new pilot friend and the man's wickedly infectious grin, John couldn't bring the world to its knees with just his smile.

"You could have done that when I walked in here." Liam waited a calculated beat before adding, "But I guess you were busy."

"Yeah." He glanced over to find Aaron gone and admitted to his lover, "I guess I was."

Thankfully, Dwight picked just that moment to storm back toward them. "They wouldn't tell me squat."

"You shouldn't be surprised," Liam, still eyeing John, informed his father. "If John couldn't milk it out of them, nobody could."

Dwight ignored the barb, having much more important battles to weigh. "'She's stable.' 'They're working on her.' 'Somebody will be out to see us soon as they can.'" The father mocked bitterly. "Same old, same old. Figured they would have come up with some new lines in the last five years."

John's heart winced. He had forgotten it had been only a short time since Liam's mother had died in a car accident. Having another beloved innocent near the brink again must be a particular kind of hell for the Taskers. John stepped over to the patriarch and gripped the man's shoulder in assurance. "This is different, Dwight. I swear to you."

"Believe him, Dad." Liam's voice cracked. "He can't lie worth shit."

Plastering on a paper-thin innocence, John intentionally goaded his bastard of a lover, "Where the hell is Aaron, anyway?"

"That your soldier friend?" Dwight relaxed slightly. "I need to thank him."

Liam wrenched out a smile so cordial and over-sweetened that John would bet it could rot dentures. "Yeah, I need to have a talk with him too." Taking a pointed look at his significant other, Liam added, "Popular guy, that Aaron. Isn't he, John?"

John waited patiently for Liam to stomp his feet and turn blue from holding his breath. "You going to stick gum in my hair, too?"

"Cereal, children?" Aaron interrupted with his arms full of a new horde of flaked goodness. And, damn the man, he flashed that ingratiating grin before his gentle gaze zeroed in on Dwight. "Any word on your daughter, sir?"

"No, son." The endearment simply slipped from the older man's tongue. He offered his outstretched hand. "I want to thank you for all you did for my girl."

Shaking the father's hand warmly, Aaron answered, "I was just lucky enough to be at the right place at the right time."

John shook his head in amusement. "Your hero complex is showing again, soldier."

"And yours could use a little daylight, doctor," Aaron replied easily.

"Both of you, I owe everything to." Dwight Tasker laid a trembling hand each on the men's arms. "Thank you, boys."

Clearing his throat to regain the attention he had lost to the so-called heroes, Liam tugged on John's soiled shirtsleeve. "I hear they're giving away free showers. Don't you think it's time you take them up on their offer, honey?"

"'Honey'?" John ground out, trying his best not to fall back on the kill option. He didn't *do* endearments. Liam didn't *do* endearments. The act of provocation was clear and uncalled for. Carefully removing Liam's fingers from his shirt, John whispered in a heated breath, "Don't push me, Liam."

"Don't push me, John." Liam's smile was feral.

"All right, let's zip up those dicks, gentlemen, and put away the rulers," Aaron softly commanded, as he handed out cardboard boxes of cereal. "There'll be plenty of time for measuring essentials once you two get home. Got it?"

Liam looked affronted.

Dwight appeared nonplussed.

John simply laughed.

Well satisfied with the responses, Aaron continued, "Good. Now, I heard an old lady by X-ray is trading boxes of Choco-Wheat Puffs for chocolate bars. What do you say we pool our grain and clear out her candy jar?"

With a skeptical brow, Dwight asked of the chief conspirator, "John said you were a soldier, son?"

"Reconnaissance," John provided with a gleam.

A scouring glance at John promised messy retribution at the eager hands of a certain pilot. "Yes. I am a soldier. Air Force." Aaron tried his best to clear things up. "And no, not reconnaissance. I was just yanking John's chain, sir."

Liam snorted. The crude smirk was expected. "And did you enjoy that *yanking*, John?"

"Enough!" Dwight Tasker growled, his ire at the moment directed solely to his son. "Do I have to remind you that you've got a sister back there who may be fighting for her life? Do you care one red cent about her? Because if you do, boy, you sure as heck are forgetting to show it." The anger on the old man's face melted away into something simply sad. "I hate to say it, but right now I think your mama would be ashamed of you."

His father's words clearly hit Liam hard. Suddenly looking more like a whipped puppy than a spurned lover, John felt honestly sorry for him—and guilty. A lead weight settled in the doctor's gut. A hell of a lot of this fiasco was John's own fault and he knew it. The problem was admitting it. He had just opened his mouth to man up to his part when Dwight moved his crosshairs squarely to his forehead.

"Don't think you don't have some explaining to do yourself, Johnny," the wounded father said. "In the middle of the night, you ran out on my boy. You might have had a good reason, I don't know, but right now that don't matter a spit to me. You showed my son no respect leaving like that. And though he don't act like it now," his laser beam gaze flashed momentarily to the bowed head of his still cowed son, "Liam was worried for you. He dragged me out of bed to help go find you." His voice fell into a whisper, haunting in its utter sadness. "I left Licia alone for that."

John found he could hardly speak. Fighting the despair threatening to overtake him, he was finally able to mutter a weak, "I am sorry."

Dwight could only shake his head. "I know you two need to talk, but I don't want to hear it. Not now. Not here. That's all I'm going to ask either one of you."

From above, there was a rush of static as the loudspeaker suddenly clicked on, bringing the whole chaotic room to an eerie standstill. The tinny voice slowly creaked out, "Would the family of Licia Tasker please come to the reception desk?" Then, in equally garish burst of static, the voice was swallowed up again into the silence.

Dwight paled and reached out for his son.

Liam caught his father's flailing arm and held on tight. "It's good news, Dad," he assured with a rock-steady calm. "It has to be."

Dwight looked up at Liam and drew from the hardened strength his son now showed in his eyes. Slowly, Dwight pulled himself back up to full height. Nodding once to Liam, he said, "Let's go, son."

The young doctor watched them weave their way through the mulling crowds with a heavy heart and a conscience all too guilty.

John Castle felt lost.

Again, the reassuring hand that had guided him through the terror of the storm returned to his neck and held tight.

* * *

"Dr. Castle? Are you all right, Doctor?"

At the sound of the nervous female voice, John looked up confusingly to find the hospital aide gripping his shoulder as she stood unsurely in front of his bent form.

"Can I get you some water?" she asked.

John almost laughed and asked the poor girl, "Got any cereal on you?" He cupped his hand over his mouth just before that incriminating piece of proof to his imminent insanity slipped out. Pushing himself back up to a more respectable sitting position, John shook his head kindly. "No water. Thank you."

"I was able to weed out some of these forms for you, Doctor. I'm afraid there's still quite a few that need your attention." She was sitting beside him again, a look of practiced encouragement in her spectacled eyes. "But I think we can get this all done in 15 minutes, tops. Then I won't bother you again, I promise."

John hoped she was well paid. She deserved every penny of it. Pulling out a paper smile from his trunk of bedside manners, John took the pile of forms from her hands. "Before we start, is there any place around here where a man can get a chocolate bar?"

* * *

"Sit down. Give me your Choco-Wheat Pops, and I'll get you that chocolate bar." It was all Aaron could think to say, and he thought it was fairly coherent for the morning they were all having. Too bad the good doctor wasn't following along.

"Huh?" The intelligence just flowed beautifully out of John's mouth.

"Sit." Aaron decided to make it as simple as possible, even giving John a firm nudge down to the empty seat.

John fell as commanded, but his desperately wounded eyes took all the joy out of Aaron's little win.

Easing himself down beside him, Aaron leaned forward over his knees to get a better angle at John's stricken face. He sighed when he saw John was honestly hurting. There were several ways Aaron could handle this situation, and being a hard ass seemed the quickest path to ultimate victory. Slowly shaking his head in sad disappointment, he accused, "You really that stupid, John?"

John squinted up his dark green eyes trying to gain some comprehension. "What?" he asked.

Aaron played the flabbergasted card. "You seriously think what happened to Licia is your fault, don't you?" When John simply dropped his gaze, Aaron declared heatedly, "You're an idiot!"

John shot back, "Why? Because I'm man enough to shoulder blame?"

"No, because you yell at me for my hero complex, while all the time you're riding around playing cowboy on your own God complex."

"Playing cowboy?" John repeated idly, obviously trying to sidetrack the discussion that was zeroing in a little too close to the truth for the doctor's comfort. "Careful, your western roots are showing," he added snidely.

A slow smile crept lecherously across Aaron's lips. "Hit it right on the head, didn't I? It's all about control."

John kept his mouth noticeably shut.

"Hate to tell you this, doc, but I doubt your measly existence had a fucking thing to do with that tornado." Aaron leaned over and grabbed John's knee in a nasty grip. Using the captured knee as a support, Aaron stuck his face right into John's and hissed, "You are not God. Hell, you're not even Mother Nature's boy toy. You're nothing in the grand scheme of things and that bugs the shit out of your ego." He thumped John hard on the chest to drive home the point to the clueless idiot. "Manning up, John, means you're admitting you're a man." Aaron slowly leaned back. "And just a man."

A dead calm spread through the green of John's eyes. "Come here," he demanded in a voice devoid of all emotion. Without waiting for a response, John stood up and stalked down a side corridor.

Aaron was immediately on his heels.

* * *

Every hospital had one. It was nearly cliché. But the storage room at the end of the hall would serve John's purposes perfectly.

Of course, the door was unlocked.

Barreling inside, John quickly took in his newest surroundings. The metal shelves that lined the walls of the small room were filled with paper supplies and cleaning liquids. A janitorial bucket complete with mop and broom sat in the corner. A quick glance at the door assured John that there was indeed an inside lock. It was perfect.

* * *

Aaron hated the sound of wet sneakers on linoleum. It was worse than fingernails on a chalkboard. The *squish-squish-squeak* stood his nerves on end and got him antsy. John was freaking lucky Aaron wasn't armed. Absently scratching his itchy trigger finger, he was about ready to jump out of his skin when John finally turned into a narrow doorway at the very end of the corridor.

A vision of Little Red Riding Hood blithely following Grandma Wolf into a closet had him musing, *My, how isolated your room is, John.* He almost said it aloud but figured the good doctor already had enough ammunition to fuel the beat-down Aaron was sure John was about to dole out to him. No need to throw lighting fluid on the doc's little sanctimonious bonfire. So Aaron kept his mouth shut, his hood firmly down over his gut instincts and blithely followed John inside.

John waited until Aaron stood in the middle of the room before he very purposefully and very slowly eased the metal door closed. John smiled as the lock clicked shut. Dull green fire raged in his eyes as he took a carefully measured step into Aaron's face. The words came out more as a snarl than speech. "Nobody talks to me like that."

Ignoring the storm of electricity John's proximity was sparking in the lowest part of his belly, Aaron swallowed calmly and looked John straight in the eye. "And maybe that's your problem." He took a step closer, close enough to feel John's warm and fast breath on his lips as he taunted, "Thank God you met me."

Without sparing an instant for sanity's sake, John rammed his forearm into Aaron's throat and shoved him hard back against the storage room's far wall. The metal shelves around them rattled at the force of the soldier's body impacting the drywall. Breathing raggedly, sweat blistering up on his forehead, John didn't loosen the pressure of his arm on Aaron's neck as he kept Aaron immobile and silent. John hissed in his face, "This isn't about God. This is about your damned mouth and the shit it's spewing."

Letting up the pressure just enough to allow Aaron to speak proved to be an error of sheer arrogance.

Before John knew what was happening, Aaron grabbed the arm at his throat and, in a practiced move of a seasoned soldier, wrenched it around John's back. Levering it up higher and higher against John's spine, Aaron didn't let up on the bone-breaking pressure until John admitted to the pain with a groan.

Keeping him pinned firmly in front of him, Aaron whispered over the trapped doctor's shoulder, "Time for a little show and tell." With each word, Aaron ratcheted back up the pressure of his hold. "This is control. One on one. Intentional. Manipulative. Taking what you want." Breathing jaggedly, his body pressed hard against John's, Aaron ground out in frustration, "You didn't do any of this kind of shit to Liam, to his father or to that little girl. You didn't manipulate. You didn't intend. You sure as hell didn't take what you wanted." Aaron shifted his grip, hoping John couldn't feel what it was Aaron's cock wanted. "You walked out and that's all. What they did after is not your fault. You. Had. No. Control." Releasing his hold, Aaron shoved him away. "Now, deal with it."

Not giving a damn about the shabby lock, Aaron flung the door open, slamming it back against the wall. As he stormed down the corridor, his sneakers squishing on the linoleum, only one thought kept blaring over and over in his head: *Ah, hell. Now I really want to fuck him.*

* * *

"No control," John Castle whispered and watched his heated breath play on the chilled windowpane. It was always so cold in waiting rooms in Florida. He supposed it was meant to be refreshing, a comforting cool away from the virulent Gulf sun. When your heart was already frozen in fear, though, cold skin did nothing more than mock the grief within.

John tiredly rubbed his eyes, trying to banish the philosophical turn his thoughts continued to make. He needed to think about this logically, in hard terms and harder numbers, then he could—

Windowpane.

Chapter Five

Water

There was a buzz all around him. Half conversations and halfhearted admonitions fell on his half-deaf ears as women in white coats shuffled him off to a hastily arranged gurney. People were pawing at him, everyone so interested in the blood escaping in dark, little droplets from his hand.

Five stitches he had guessed right from the start, right from the moment his fist met glass and bled. He decided to say it aloud, to add his voice to the cacophony of useless noise that now littered his world. "Five. Two across the knuckles, and one of those might be tricky. Then three on the forefinger. Easy."

They ignored him, as well they should have, as he was the idiot who had just shoved his hand through a window; although, to his utter consternation and embarrassment, one nurse dared to pat him on the head. That alone was his saving grace from the cocktail of sedatives that was being bantered about for the "poor, distraught fellow." It was this condescending pet that was just enough to irk him out of his self-inflicted stupor.

"I'm a doctor, you know!" he loudly declared as he scruffed his uninjured hand through his hair, patting *up* what she had just patted *down*. "And I didn't throw my head through the window so there's no need in you touching my hair." He sounded rude and indignant and Aaron would have laughed himself silly at his self-aggrandizing—and it was just what he needed to feel like John Castle again.

He took a deep breath and dragged out his best bedside manner for the staff. "Why don't you just stitch me up and I'll get out of your hair? It was a stupid reaction that won't happen again. I'll promise you that."

"Why did you do it?" A nurse too young to be safely off of breast milk foolishly asked.

There was a collective moan from the more senior of the nursing staff.

John, though, had tired of the anger and settled back into a weary exhaustion as he laid out the ugly truth. "My best friend was shot twice tonight. He'll probably die. Reason enough?"

No one had much to say after that.

* * *

The Georgia sky was a dangerous blue, mesmerizing and cold. It would lure your eye into its endless beauty while its frigid fingers would take an unrelenting grip of your heart. Then, when your last breath was taken and so innocently released, the sole thought in your mind would be, "Wow! Now, isn't that pretty?"

It was skies like these that made Aaron yearn for a plane. With wings under his feet, he'd tear the heavenly sea apart, and ride on its white-capped waves into the sun.

Where was he instead? He was stuck in fucking Columbus, Georgia, with not so much as a crop duster in sight. Not to mention the hard-on he was lugging around, just another infuriating throttle he couldn't, at the moment, lay hands on to fly.

Scathing conversation aside, the up close and personal tête-à-tête with John in the storage room had been, and was still, physically infuriating. His body kept making leaps and bounds about his sexuality that his mind was in no way ready to contemplate, let alone act on. Case in point: when John had full-body pressed him against the wall, his cock had jumped to attention with a speed that quite frankly knocked all his thinking parts for a dizzying loop. What was the result of this sexual vertigo? He would have let the man fuck him right then and there. It was that realization alone that had driven him to turn on John, to take the control back, and if he got to shove a little bit of the man's ego right back down his throat, so be it. A smile tickled Aaron's lips at that.

While hiding one consternation with his coat, Aaron stood now staring up at the other. He had escaped out into the daylight of the hospital's parking lot directly from the janitor's closet. He had needed air, light, and the ice-cold breath of November to simmer him down. But even now as he stood longingly looking at the sky, his breath was still ragged and his body was still distracted—so distracted, in fact, that Aaron barely felt the brush against his arm when a man rushed past him. The figure began heaving into the azalea bushes as he fell hard onto his knees. It wasn't until the man rose up for a gulp of fresh air that Aaron recognized the agonized being as Liam Tasker. Aaron rushed immediately to the man's side.

"Mr. Tasker?" Aaron held on to the convulsing shoulders, whispering tightly in his ear. "Please, sir? What's wrong?" Horrific thoughts flooded Aaron's already over-imaginative brain. So, as no answer was given for long minutes as Dwight continued to vomit, Aaron thought seriously of joining him in the activity. He shook Dwight's arm a little more urgently. "Please, Mr. Tasker."

Ever so slowly, the convulsions came to an end and the man raised himself up trembling from the ground. He looked at Aaron with the eyes of a dead man as he confided, "They thought she'd lose her arm."

"What?" Aaron stood stunned for a tortuous moment until his tongue decided to rejoin the game, "No," he argued. "No way." Little girls, no matter what they went through, should always be fine. The stark look on Dwight's face, however, easily told Aaron it was the truth. Running both his hands through his hair, then over his face, Aaron scrubbed off the initial shock and requested calmly, "Tell me what they said."

The wrinkles that creased Dwight's face grew deeper as he tried to come up with the proper terms, "They called it a meta—"

Aaron reached out and touched the man's arm gently. He asked with no shame, "In your words, sir. Please. I don't know any more than you do."

With a grateful but weary sigh, Dwight delved into a long story of crushed bone, severed nerves, and impeded blood flow. Despite the layman terminology, the medical tale was still a gruesome one. The end, however, miraculously turned out to be a happy one.

"They didn't think it would work. They had all the instruments right there and ready to take off my little girl's arm… it was so close, son. But God had other ideas than to make my Licia a cripple. She's been blessed."

"And so have you." Aaron smiled and Dwight simply nodded his head in silent affirmation. "So she'll be okay? She'll have full use of her arm and everything?"

"They think so. A miracle is what one of them called it. The other is already talking about writing up an article about it for some medical journal."

"No disrespect, sir, but I don't think I'll be reading it." Aaron scrunched up his face, easily imagining the gory details and possible visuals.

"Me neither, Aaron." Dwight winked conspiratorially at him. "We lived it and that's more than enough, I think."

"Me too." The grin, though tired, was still infectious. "It's been one heck of a day, sir."

"It's a heck of a life, son." Dwight took in a deep, fulfilling breath and looked up at the sky. "And it is a beautiful day."

Aaron looked back up into the blue that no longer mocked him and smiled. "It is that."

* * *

John Castle was stymied. He wasn't even sure of the exact definition of the word but he knew he was stymied, and he knew that in all of his 23 years he had never been stymied before.

Damn that pushy bastard.

Kicking the door shut with his foot, John sat cross-legged down on the storage room's floor. Since he physically couldn't kick the shit out of himself, John decided he needed to ruminate on some things.

"Ruminate?" John snickered to the mop and its bucket. "What the hell has that S.O.B. done to my head?"

The discomfiture of another part of his anatomy also made itself known. Staring down at his scrunched but happy-go-lucky hard-on, he kicked out one leg to his side to give the troublemaker some more room. "Now shut up and let me think."

God, he was tired. The world swam before him in a haze of exhaustion and guilt. Dropping his head to rest on his upturned knee, John let his eyes drift close. The marks of Aaron's fingers on his arm throbbed in a dull recitation of his heartbeat. He let the pain lull him into a bliss of sweet nothingness.

He didn't know how long he stayed there like that, but as he raised his head back up and opened his once again bright eyes to the world, John was no longer stymied.

He was just well and royally fucked.

* * *

They had moved him. Once he'd been stitched back together again and duly chastised by staff and security alike, John had been escorted with kid gloves to a small surgical waiting room in the east wing of the Florida hospital. There were no windows in this room.

At least the pain had been well worth it. While

they were busy trying to find a place for him to safely stay and not self-destruct, they had calmed him by sending a nurse with some pull to the operating room to get a no-shit update on Aaron.

The news had, indeed, been straightforward and overall good—that is, good for a man with two bullets in him. Aaron Chambers was still alive and holding his own through the first hours of surgery. John could have needled some more details out of the nurse but knowing more would only make him think more. Thinking more was unacceptable, since John was already stymied.

The small waiting room, for some unfathomable reason, had a large dictionary sitting on its corner table. John thumbed through it now with his good hand, looking for the definition that had eluded him all these years.

He found it on page 637: "Stymied: a verb meaning to be thwarted or stumped by a problem or a situation."

John laughed sourly at the simplicity of those words. Maybe *stymied* had never been the right word? Maybe *fucked*, all along, had been the right choice?

Carefully, John laid the tome back down and wiped all mundane thoughts of words and their proper usages from his overtaxed brain. From now on, only two words would matter in his world: survival and revenge.

* * *

John walked out of the Georgia storage room and right into a fist.

Fortunately for the doctor's teeth, Liam's aim was off and the punch ended up *merely* a glancing blow to the cheekbone.

It still hurt like crap, though. "Shit, Liam!" Bending over, John gingerly cupped his face. He hissed, "What the fuck do you think you're doing?"

"Something I should have done when I caught you making doe eyes at that damned soldier yesterday." Doe eyes? Maybe John had been hit harder than he thought. Liam ignored John's vigorous shaking of his head and raged on, "A good old-fashioned butt-kicking would have saved us all, especially Licia, a hell of a lot of hurt."

Straightening up, John leveled his shoulders, a knee-jerk reaction to being attacked by both word and hand, but his righteous anger dwindled quickly away in the face of the remembered truth. With a long calming breath he softened the instinctual vexation in his voice and apologized, "I'm sorry I left last night. I could have handled that better...I *should* have handled that better."

"What did you handle instead, John? Air Force cock?"

John snarled, "Leave him out of this."

"Or did you finally get yourself fucked?" Liam shook his head mournfully and *tsked*. "Going to miss dreaming about that virgin hole of yours."

John could feel his face burn red, shame warring with anger. Clinching his teeth together, holding in every shitty thing he wanted to say, he finally growled out a less combative, "Shut up, Liam."

The whole of Liam's face contorted into something malicious and ugly. "Oh, I will once you get on your knees to apologize for almost killing my sister."

Unconsciously, John's fingers curled into fists, despite his wholehearted effort to remain cold and unaffected. "Where's your father?"

The question surprised him and Liam did nothing to hide his curiosity. "Why?" he asked suspiciously.

It was a battle not to go off on the man. Every affect, every mannerism of Liam's seemed to annoy the hell out of John at the moment, but he forced himself to push past all that. There was only one thing he needed to know. Taking a deep breath, John said as calmly as he could, "Because I'm not trusting a word that comes out of your mouth right now, and I have got to know that little girl is all right."

Recognizing the sincerity in John's appeal, Liam sobered just long enough for the two necessary words, "She is." Tender moment over, Liam reverted to bastard mode. "No thanks to you and your wandering dick, but she is all right."

In a sigh of utter relief, John replied, "Thank God."

Liam laughed nastily. "Yeah, God… not you."

It was meant to be an insult, another slap in the face, but to John it was simply affirming. "You're right. Not me." He was sure the little quirk of a smile he gave Liam as he walked away confused the hell out of the man, but John didn't give a shit. He had a pilot to find.

Locating Aaron became a long, protracted tour of all of the ins and outs of the Columbus, Georgia, hospital. By the time he had exhausted every nook and cranny inside, John's countenance had turned foul. He was sure he was sporting a damn fine scowl as he spotted his quarry leaning against a light post outside looking edible.

John doubted there were many people who could pull off the tornado-ravaged look with such effortless success. The scowl he had been sporting only moments before fled in the presence of such rough-edged delight. John rolled his eyes at the thought, nearly tripping over a bumper in the process.

Apparently that had been just enough awkward movement to catch Aaron's eye. He grinned cockily as John limped closer.

John should have been pissed, but he found himself instead inordinately relieved that the tension stoked in the storage room hadn't survived in the bright light of day. He had just opened his mouth to say something cunning, and perhaps even wicked, when he was cut off by a shout from the other direction.

"Lieutenant!" The woman's voice that carried forcefully across the parking lot was familiar, as was her strong face and even stronger stride. It was an eerie sense of *déjà vu* for John, and he briefly wondered who it was that needed rescuing this time.

Sergeant Rosalyn Campos approached them with purpose and determination—the approach she took with most things in her life, John would guess. With her long, fiery red hair pulled back into a tight ponytail, her high cheekbones and almond-shaped hazel eyes were particularly striking and disarming. John could imagine many an enemy combatant struck nervously dumb at the first sight of her; it was an advantage of which he was sure the soldier took full use.

Aaron viewed her unexpected arrival with obvious worry. He crinkled up his nose and nervously wiped his mouth as he watched her hurried approach. "Do I want to know?" he asked as soon as she was within earshot.

"No, sir." To John's utter amazement, she somehow twinkled those hazel eyes of steel at Aaron.

Aaron, however, was not impressed. Rolling his eyes in hard-won impatience, he waved the military endearment off. "Can the 'sir,' Ro."

Standing in a relaxed at-ease posture, she quirked the corner of her lip into a smirk born to infuriate. "I thought this was an off week, sir. But I could check my calendar?"

Aaron failed miserably at stifling a chuckle. "Just tell me and stop trying to smile. You know it gives me the willies."

"Yes, sir."

"Sergeant!" Aaron roared in just right the tenor to get the girl moving.

It worked. Sergeant Rosalyn Campos automatically stood straighter, all humor gone from her eyes as she reported, "The base got a hold of Beck. You both have got new orders." She lost eye contact for only a moment before she finished, completely composed, "We lost a transport over the Gulf. Seven casualties, two of them fatalities. They need you and Beck there tonight."

The pilot didn't so much as blink an eye. "You told them about..." He waved his hand around them, signifying the clusterfuck that surrounded them at the moment.

"Yes, sir," she replied with a trace of defeat in her

otherwise emotionless voice. "They've made the arrangements for you to ship out from Atlanta. We've got transportation. We need to go, sir."

"I hear you, Sergeant." He looked around him, his gaze lingering briefly on the doctor. "One hour." Aaron saw her start to object and quickly cut her off. "I'm not going anywhere until I shower this crap off, Ro."

She quirked a wry smile as she appraised his state of filth. "Excellent strategy, sir."

"Smart mouth," he easily called her on her bitchiness.

A flicker of something akin to fire blossomed in the far back of her eyes, "If this wasn't an off week, sir"—she let the last linger ever so treacherously on the tip of her tongue—"I'd make a scathing retort."

Aaron's smile grew flame of its own, as he cocked his head alluringly to the side, "I'm sure you would." He let the silence dance softly between them for just a moment. "Now, get out of here. I'll meet you in the lobby in 60."

"Yes, sir." She soldiered off with a little more sway in her hips than John suspected was necessary; it even took his gaze a long while to break contact.

Dwight Tasker strolled up from behind them, an appreciative whistle on his lips. "Pretty girl. That one your fiancée, Aaron?"

John began to laugh.

But Aaron shocked the hell out of him by saying, "Yep." After a sideways glance at a gaping John, he quickly modified, "On and off. *Off* this week, apparently."

John was numb, the kind of numb that vibrates in your skull. He just stood there and stared.

The kitty-cat prowess of Liam paid off again. Nearly scaring the living daylights out of John, he gleamed suddenly over his shoulder. "Lucky girl, wouldn't you say, love?"

John was going to puke.

Aaron swept in and rescued him with a simple request. "I've got to get this grime off me before I head out. John, do you think you could use some of those doctoring credentials to find me a spare shower?"

"I'll see what I can do." It was, after all, just what John needed. He needed to get away, a moment to digest, and this was as good a chance as any.

* * *

Liam barely waited for John to take the first step away, before he looked at his father with a plastered on grin. "They've got Licia in a room now. We can see her."

Life flooded back into the old man's withered eyes. "Why didn't you say something?" He gave his son an excited slug on the shoulder as his dentures beamed in the daylight. "Should be shouting news like that to the skies."

Liam's mouth creased into the basics of a smile. "You go first, Dad. I want to get her some flowers from that florist we saw down the block." Seeing his father about to disagree, Liam added with a bit more heart, "Maybe they've got some of her daisies."

Dwight Tasker wasn't a fool. He knew whatever Liam was up to was most likely bastardly. He took a hard look at Aaron and decided right away the young soldier could easily take whatever Liam could dole out. In fact, whatever was left of his firstborn would most likely be dog-ugly. Turning back to his eldest, Dwight offered his boy one final out. "You sure, son?"

"Oh yes, very sure." He nodded without a shred of doubt or a morsel of common sense. "I'll be up there in a bit."

"Okay," Dwight shrugged, giving up. He had a little girl inside he really needed to see. Before he left, however, there was one thing he had to clear up. Turning to Aaron, Dwight laid a hand on his shoulder. "Did I hear that girl right? You're fixing to leave?"

"Yes, sir."

"Sorry to hear that," Dwight said truthfully, before giving the boy a departing smile. "Come see me before you take off. I might have thought of the words by then to properly thank you." Before Aaron could open his mouth to respond, Dwight shuffled hurriedly away.

"Seems like you've got the whole world wrapped around your finger." The snide comment rolled off of Liam's tongue with a surprisingly practiced ease.

Aaron rolled his eyes, really starting to hate this jerk. "I don't have the time for this." With a growing need for restraint, Aaron didn't so much as brush Liam's shadow as he started to make his way by him.

Liam had other plans for him. In a foolhardy and awkward move, Liam somehow managed to swerve right back into Aaron's path, blocking his way. Cockily positioning his fists on his hips, oddly resembling a turtle-necked pirate, grandiosely Liam snarled, "You are going to make the time."

Aaron stifled the overwhelming urge to laugh.

Liam caught the effort and struck back with a cheer-infused venom. "I saw you jerking off to me and John."

Aaron paled but stood his ground and waited for the barrage.

Liam was quite happy to oblige. "Oh, wait! That's right." He looked like a cat who just spotted a lame canary. "You didn't even have to do the jerking. You just blew hands-free like some kind of fucking pervert." He took a step back, crossed his arms across his chest, and chuckled. "Bet you haven't told your new pal John about that. Am I wrong?"

Aaron stared him down, sheer willfulness disguising the inner turmoil of the man. While Liam might have correctly surmised Aaron's embarrassment, however, Liam had greatly miscalculated the amount of guilt involved in that shame: none. In a mild tone, Aaron dared, "Tell him."

"What?" Liam's gaze turned suspicious, his brain busily churning away trying to figure out the soldier's strategy. "What did you say?"

A casual twitch of his shoulders made it clear that Aaron didn't mind repeating, "You heard me. You tell him, or I will." It took all of his will power to look away from the flummoxed man, but Aaron forced his attention to a particularly itchy scratch on his left hand. He added without looking up, "Bet you won't like his reaction."

Aaron could just hear all the various possibilities churning through Liam's head, with only a very few of them ending with "happily ever after." Liam bristled. "You're bluffing."

Scratch-scratch-scratch. Aaron's thumbnail casually worked at the reddened skin on the back of his hand. "I don't bluff. Don't need to." Aaron stopped his scratching to chuckle. "Now, how cliché is that? Bet your pal John will get a real kick out of it."

An angry flush flooded Liam's cheeks as he struck out at the potentially new soft spot, "And your soldier-girl? What about her?"

An off-putting amusement played in Aaron's eyes as he baited the jerk, "Call her that to her face. I double-dog dare you."

His face shriveled into something ugly and crazy. "I could kill you."

Aaron did laugh at that, but only briefly, before lacing his next words with ice. "And I could rip out your fucking throat." Aaron stared down at his own feet. They shuffled back and forth innocently in the gravel, as if such threats were commonplace in his life, almost taxing to his interest. Finally, he sighed and shrugged apologetically. "But I won't. It would be stupid. You may be a whiny, snot-nosed brat, but I know you're not stupid either."

They both caught sight of John approaching at the same time. He was in a hurry as he crossed the parking lot, unfortunately giving neither one of them time to satisfactorily conclude their chat. They only had a few moments before their mutual friend would be within easy earshot.

Liam jumped first. Attempting to stand normal, attempting to look totally blasé, Liam sounded anything but casual as he demanded in a heated rush, "What are you going to do?"

"Keep you guessing." To describe the look on Aaron's face would be to define the phrase "dastardly innocence." Aaron wore the look remarkably well, and kept it on as John approached.

* * *

John, for his part, didn't suspect a thing, as he was still mulling over the Rosalyn news. "I got you a shower," he said, but the explanation of how this had occurred came with a put-upon frown. "The head surgeon's got a private bathroom. I had to brown-nose my ass off for you, so you'd better enjoy every drop of that damned water."

"Ahhh! The heart of a doctor is ever so giving." Aaron clapped John on the shoulder as he took off at a jog back toward the hospital. "Thanks," he called out over his back just before he disappeared inside.

Just wondering, Liam asked, "Does he know where—"

"He's going? Not a clue."

"And he flies planes?" Liam couldn't hide his amusement.

John joined in the lightheartedness with a very serious nod. "My faith in the U.S. government is steadily rising."

Liam had relaxed enough to actually chuckle at that.

John watched his lover a moment before asking, "Are we okay?"

"*We*?" Liam snorted with a disappointed shake of his head. "Wrong pronoun, John. *You and me* would be more appropriate, don't you think?"

Keeping a corner of his eye on the hospital door, knowing Aaron would come scurrying out of it any moment, John thought it was time to be brutally honest. "I think it's pretty much always been a case of *you and me*. We played at the *we*."

Liam nodded slowly as melancholy mixed with wistfulness. "We played it well."

"From time to time, we did." The small smile that had found a reluctant home on John's face fled as he watched Liam's reaction to the hospital's door being flung open. Bitterness swelled out of every pore as Liam spotted Aaron. John's decision was made. His words were quick but firm in stating what they both already knew. "Playtime's over."

As he watched John jog toward a clearly perturbed Air Force pilot, Liam smiled grimly as he agreed, "Yes, it is."

* * *

Sometime the sun had set. The little field of Florida sunshine that had filled a corner of the outer hallway had disappeared without even a goodbye. John rearranged his ever-tiring body in the ill-thought-out seat and decided maybe avoiding any goodbyes was in the end a good idea. So he decided not to miss the sun or its light. He'd catch them again tomorrow.

Thoughts of tomorrow brought on thoughts to the actual time. He didn't have his watch on; it still sat, he supposed, on the patio table next to his empty bottle of beer, but thoughts of his home, *their* home, could not be allowed right now. He had to stay in the present or escape into the more distant past. Yesterdays and todays were simply toxic to his sanity. So he would stay clear of those minefields until he knew Aaron was going to heal and Liam Tasker was going to die.

The clock on the waiting room's wall struck 12:00, and today turned into tomorrow without even a goodbye.

* * *

The age of the hospital had never crossed Aaron's mind until he stepped into the chief of surgery's private bathroom. It was vintage, to put a kind word to it. Cold could be another word. Sanitary would probably be the best word. Everything from the subway tiles on the wall to the honeycombed tile floor, the pedestal sink, and the two wall sconces hanging beside its square mirror was a frigid white. Aaron felt a chill just looking into the place, and the thought of getting naked in there was by no means warming his cockles. In fact, he could feel his cockles shriveling up at that very moment.

"Best I could do." John's voice somehow provided its own snicker and shrug, but Aaron refused to turn around and actually witness the smugness. "You know, this place could be a lot worse." John played the "Aren't you a haughty bastard?" card to perfection.

Aaron countered as best as anyone could: he simply agreed. "Yep, it could be worse. It could be pink with little bunnies everywhere. That would just about freeze my balls off as fast as this."

With hands stuffed casually in his jeans pockets and a smart-ass look on his face, John joined Aaron in the doorway. After a moment's thought, John defended the bathroom's honor. "It's clean."

"Sterile."

John, though, could be a stubborn bastard and wasn't about to let his defense go down without a fight. "You could eat a steak off that floor."

Aaron surrendered to the laughter. "And that thought is wrong on so many levels."

"Shut up and strip." The pitch of John's voice dropped to a level stupefying for most brain cells and electrifying for all dicks.

Aaron shook himself out of the stupor and taunted to cover his fall, "Careful, John. Stuff like that is why Liam hates your guts."

"He hates your guts too," John was quick and disproportionately gleeful to point out.

"Yeah, but I'm not fucking him."

"Neither am I. Not any more." John's face took on an unreadable quality.

Suddenly indignant to the point of being flustered, Aaron jabbed his finger at John. "Now, that is not my fault!"

John just looked down at his feet and shrugged. "Didn't say it was."

Aaron studied the man hard. John looked placid. It was a good look for the doctor. Aaron tore his eyes away and bent down to untie his shoes. "Explains why Liam went all kamikaze on me out there."

"He's all talk." John sounded so sure.

"Not all talk." A steamy vision of Liam on his knees sucking off John like he was the last popsicle in the Sahara quickly flashed before Aaron's eyes. Aaron immediately misdirected that rising line of thought by pointing at John's growing shiner. "He missed, or you ducked?"

"Not all of us can be lethal weapons with nice packages." John's eyes drifted south. And stayed.

It was blatant. Apparently the time for being circumspect was inching to a close, and Aaron found to his utter discomfort that he was enjoying it. So, being a coward with an overactive dick but a scared shitless mind, Aaron scurried back from that invisible line by bringing the girlfriend needlessly into the conversation. "Do I need to get Rosalyn in here?" he joked with a smile that kept slipping over that freaking thin border into the flirtatious.

John paused for a heartbeat, as if deciding which of two paths to follow. In the end, he retreated from the line and asked behind a mask of polite interest, "What is the story there?"

"I love her." No hesitation was needed for the answer. It was simply truth. Aaron took off his dirty left sock and threw it in the immaculate corner.

"Yeah, and she loves you, so?" John tried for flippant but backtracked into bitter. Catching his mistake, John cleared his throat and tried the casual line again, "I mean, why is it *off*?"

That path-choosing dilemma of John's was suddenly delivered onto Aaron. Hard-core or soft porn? Or, in other words, the truth or a joke? To hell with it. Aaron always liked it rough. "I'm her commanding officer. It gets…" He paused, realizing that maybe the brutal honesty wasn't going to be as clear cut as he hoped. He sighed and went for the first word that had popped into his head. "It gets weird, sometimes." He dropped his eyes, fingering a string on his right sock. "For both of us, I know it gets weird."

"Against regulations?" John guessed.

Aaron tore off his other sock. "That's not the problem." He threw the offending stocking across the room. It landed by its partner. What the hell was he doing? This was a mistake. He had to get out of this. "Sorry about…" Aaron trailed off with a jerk of his head downstairs to signify Liam without actually having to say the creep's name. He left the apology there, hoping that would be enough of a stick for John to chase after.

John, however, decided to play the gentleman. He graciously waved off Aaron's efforts of lukewarm apology. "Like you said, not your fault."

"How long?" He hadn't meant to ask, but he did. His belt followed his socks in the same vein of frustration.

John stuffed his hands once again into his pockets, as he leaned back against the pedestal sink. "Six months."

Aaron nodded slowly. "Three years," he offered for no good reason at all.

"Off and on," John reminded him softly.

"Yeah." Unconsciously, Aaron reached for the top button of his jeans. It was consciously that he stopped. Leaving his hand on his fly, Aaron didn't dare look up at John as he waited.

"Yeah," John repeated in much the same resigned tone as Aaron's sigh. With a twist of his hip, he pushed himself off the sink and headed for the door. "I'll let you get to it. See you downstairs."

"Thanks," Aaron called out lamely just as the door slammed shut between the two men.

* * *

John would forever wonder what had possessed him. Sense, decorum, just basic human courtesy had obviously flown out his mind's window while John's dick had been ogling Aaron as he oh-so slowly disrobed. In that case, he supposed, he could claim loss of sanity.

Ah, hell, whatever the legal defense John Castle was guilty. He saw something he wanted but couldn't have, so he took it. He really ought to have felt like a grade-A bastard as he swung that bathroom door back open, but all John felt at that moment and all that he would feel looking back at it would be a sense of Fate. Trust Aaron to be the one to introduce him to the bitch.

He had waited until he heard the water running. Ear pressed to the door like a bad cliché, John had listened for the pounding of water on tile and skin. After long minutes of keen eavesdropping the water did finally come, but instead of a torrent, he heard only a trickle. The curse from inside only confirmed his conclusion that the water pressure was nil. John smiled. Following dew-shaped water drops as they coasted down the no-doubt brilliant lines of a well-packaged soldier in arms would be a delight for his eyes, not to mention other anxious parts of his anatomy. This was going to be good—that is, if "well-packaged soldier in arms" didn't kill him first.

John knew it would be worth the risk.

It was.

Swinging the door open with a confidence that bordered on idiotic bravado, John took two steps inside and re-shut the door behind him before even raising his eyes from the white tiled floor. The slow journey up to Aaron's face was a trip for which any like-minded man would gladly risk life and limb.

John's entrance had somehow remained undetected, providing the stalker with a profile shot to die for. The arch of Aaron's foot clearing the slowly swirling puddle of water as it fell down the drain captured John's eye first. From a strong ankle came a calf muscle both hard and lithe. Continuing up the silk field of perfect skin, John's gaze lingered on a bulging thigh, a narrow hip, and a long penis bowing down in sweet rest.

John bit his bottom lip and sucked it hard between his teeth.

The journey continued. From the nest of wet curls at his groin, the creamy, flawless skin reached upward in smooth, hairless stretches. Lying like buttery satin across his six-pack of abs, Aaron's skin rose up to embrace lean muscles and dark brown nipples. The pull of his shoulders as he stood washing his hair accentuated the keen lines of his body's perfection.

Within his own jeans, John's cock wept in fervent appreciation.

John couldn't keep quiet any longer. His voice was hard and graveled as he asked the oblivious man, "Have you ever been targeted, soldier?"

Aaron's training paid great dividends at that moment. It seemed he was surprised but only the corner of his left eye betrayed it. He remained cool, confident yet anxious for an explanation. He did not move to cover himself as he asked with a tight grin, "What kind of question is that?" He tried to laugh it off, but once he saw John was having none of it, Aaron answered seriously, "It's my life. Being targeted. Targeting. Surviving both while getting the job done." John's mouth turned to sand as Aaron dropped one hand to his hip. Aaron's penis bobbed as he moved.

Parched but ever vigilant, John continued to demand in husky whispers, "Do you ever lose?"

Aaron blinked, raised his brows a time or two in

confusion, then finished with a shake of his head. "I'm here, aren't I?"

"That's not an answer," John snapped.

Aaron had finally lost patience. "John, what are you getting at? I'm deploying in 30 minutes. Your fuck-buddy has already wasted ten of my minutes threatening me and my dick, and now you stroll in here asking me cryptic questions while you don't even give a fuck that I'm standing here naked and... and soapy."

"Slippery too, I bet." John's look was purely predatory. "I don't want you to lose *over there*." He flicked his eyes somewhere eastward, somewhere that transports went down and pilots were killed.

Aaron understood. One by one his muscles stood down, while his cock began to peek up. His promise came softly. "I won't."

Suddenly, John took a step toward him. He literally hissed as the hunter gave his prey a final look-over. "But I wouldn't mind you losing to some targeting stateside."

Aaron stood taller, braver. "Is that a threat?"

"Oh, yeah."

John Castle pounced.

* * *

John's eyes had turned black with need, the out-of-control hunger burning within him incinerating the green from existence. It would have been frightening, if it wasn't such an unexpected turn-on. Aaron rarely found himself the underdog in any confrontation. To be thrust into such a role now was mind-numbing and cock-tickling. The blood rushed from his head to his dick at such a reckless pace that he was left incredibly lightheaded, and he had to back up against the cold tile to brace himself up on weakened knees.

It was a good thing that John moved fast. He crossed the small bathroom in four long steps, reaching Aaron in the same breath that he had left. John's hands slapped against the subway tile on either side of Aaron's head, locking him in place, mentally if not physically.

The smell of John's sweat mingled with all the other scents of their night before so forcefully surrounding him set every one of Aaron's nerves on end. Chill blades spread across his naked skin like fire. His heart thundered in his suddenly heaving chest.

John pressed closer.

The first thing to brush his eager skin was the denim of John's right leg. John wedged itself between Aaron's legs. Greedily John shoved Aaron's left leg aside, insinuating his body within Aaron's. The inside curve of John's hipbone suddenly pushed hard into Aaron's half-risen penis. The pressure, the strength, the feel of the rough denim against the highly sensitized flesh of his shaft nearly rocketed Aaron into an orgasm of truly catastrophic heights. What little part of his brain that was still working pleaded with Aaron not to come, warned him that getting off on this would turn his life upside down. He couldn't destroy his career, his whole life for one meaningless fuck.

But then John kissed him.

The world decided to spin out of control without one spent drop of come. His mind surrendered without another peep as to duty and regulation. Every sensation that his body couldn't by the laws of science feel, his brain created and felt in blooming color.

His eyes, though closed, witnessed every morsel of John as he laid his body over Aaron's water-kissed skin.

Though the only sound was the slow raining down of the water onto the tile, Aaron could hear John's voice. There weren't words so much as presence. It was intoxicating to have another voice join his own in his ever-swirling mind. If this was craziness it was a hell of a lot better than loneliness.

The kiss lasted an eternity and more. At first, Aaron lips had remained dumb, inactive, flesh simply on which John could feed, but as Aaron's legs were marshaled wider apart, as the belt loops on John's jeans tickled his navel, as Aaron's hardened nipples became accustomed to John's sweater rubbing rug burns across its nubs, Aaron's mouth sprung to life. One of the Aaron's most favorite things in the whole of the world was kissing, and he was a master of it.

Opening his mouth just enough to lure John's tongue in, Aaron allowed John to get the feel of him. He luxuriated in the touch of tongue to teeth and gums and throat. He played passive while he learned the ridges and girth of John's tongue. When the recon was complete, Aaron smiled and bit down on the intruding appendage. John yelped in Aaron's mouth and Aaron took the planned opportunity to launch his own invasion. Pushing his tongue inside, Aaron ravaged the inner linings of John's mouth.

John's breath caught, then sped up.

The onslaught of pilot in doctor continued. Aaron could feel John's rod harden to steel as the man began to hump Aaron's naked hip.

John grabbed the back of the soldier's head, his fingers tightening in the man's hair, as he suddenly yanked Aaron's mouth away from his own. John heaved in great lungfuls of air as he slowly removed his body from Aaron's skin. "I'm never mentioning this again," he huffed out with flushed cheeks and raw, swollen lips. "Never."

A moment was taken to regain equilibrium before John removed his hand from the wall. He didn't speak again until they no longer touched. His breathing was still labored as he made Aaron understand. "I think you're a damned good man and would be proud to call you a friend. The rest is up to you." John reached into his back pocket and tossed his business card on to Aaron's stack of clothes. More steps were taken away as he backed up slowly to the door. When he reached the doorjamb, John smirked. "At least let me know that you didn't get your fucking head blown off over there."

Still relying on the wall to keep him upright, Aaron mumbled around his own battered lips, "Pilot." He dragged a breath out of his overworked lungs, as he smarted back darkly. "I'm more likely to go down in a ball of flames."

John laughed as he brushed the stray lock of hair back again from his forehead. "Then make it a pretty one, flyboy."

"Bastard," Aaron stated boldly for a man completely naked.

"Whippersnapper," John reminded as he quickly escaped out the door.

"A hell of a way to end a friendship." Aaron couldn't help but wonder at the risk John had taken. "A hell of a risk," he mouthed to the empty room.

A nervous smile claimed Aaron as he realized, *might be time for me to take some risks of my own.*

* * *

Liam Tasker knew all about risks.

Sitting out in his car in the Florida hospital's parking lot, he was taking a hell of a big one, but it was worth it.

Oh, yes, it was worth it.

Chapter Six

Rocks

The petulant tiptoeing of time through the cold, silent room was wearing John down. A bubbly nurse had bounced into his enclave an hour ago, handing out promises like brightly colored candy of an update "really soon." John had swallowed that *candy* down whole but now was left with a voracious want as the hour had passed with neither a sugared nor soured word more.

He looked down at the cold cup of coffee he held in his hands and cursed the realization that he was hungry. He'd need nourishment soon, but the thought of shoving a sandwich down his throat at the moment was vile.

He half wished the police would come back. The latest set of detectives had left about two hours ago. The same questions were asked. The same answers were given. They did ask how to spell "Liam," which John took as a positive sign that maybe they were taking his so-called hunch seriously.

John huffed indignantly as he slammed down the paper cup of swill on the coffee table. "Hunch?" he muttered to the emptiness of the room. "How is it *just* a hunch when the stupid bastard had come right out and threatened Aaron to his face?" What more could they possibly want?

The cops had quickly pointed out the fact that the threat had come nearly nine years ago, with apparently no direct interaction between the men since then.

John had quickly corrected them.

* * *

The wiles of Lady Fate that day were particularly bitchy. Nothing had gone as planned. John really shouldn't have been surprised, but there he was sitting on his checked luggage in Denver International Airport, shocked as hell.

First off, it was June and it was snowing. Sure, he knew it was Colorado but, need he repeat? It was June! For the hundredth time that week, he asked himself, "What the fuck am I doing?"

It was a legitimate question, perfectly acceptable and quite possibly necessary seeing as how he was gnawing on his nails like a fourth-grade girl. Jamming his hands under his thighs, he thought back on how he had become this sniveling idiot.

John should never have answered the phone. Granted, a call from Afghanistan in the middle of the night would pique anybody's curiosity but he should have known better. He should have known it was that annoying bastard on the other end.

It had been four years since that day in Columbus, Georgia, and he hadn't seen Aaron Chambers since, but the pilot had still somehow managed to wedge himself right into John's life. E-mails, a couple of postcards, and the occasional phone call had been just enough to cement the men's friendship. Though nothing about those few explosive minutes in the shower had ever been brought up, they had clearly not been forgotten either. Sexual innuendo still reared its pesky head in their every other word. It was a game. It was fun. It was the damned middle of the night and the bastard had better not be dead. That alone was why John answered that fateful phone call. It had all gone downhill from there.

"Hello." He remembered his own voice sounding fuzzy headed, as if sleep still held his tongue in her cunt.

"Thought I was dead again?" A throaty laughter jerked John out of her folds.

"You call just to piss me off?" He knuckled his eyes clumsily as he threw his feet over the bedside. Sure, he was glad the bastard wasn't dead, but that didn't mean he couldn't be fucking grumpy.

"Nope." Aaron sounded downright jolly. "I called with an invitation."

Fine. John would take Aaron's *cheery* and raise him one *shitty*. "Finally marrying the sergeant?"

"Have you seen Roach?" The infuriating dope deliberately misunderstood.

It was too early in the morning to get creative, though, so John just threw out a highly appropriate, "Ass."

"Sure, he's got one, but I haven't looked."

That was about all the cocky parlaying John could take before coffee. "I'm hanging up now."

"Wanna go play in the rocks with me?"

The words had all came out in a rush, and it took John a moment to correctly digest them. He was not impressed. "I see that promotion is doing wonders for your maturity." The lieutenant had turned captain only a month before.

He swept off the insult with a hyper volley of words. "Rock climbing. Colorado, in June. Two weeks, my treat. Your last fling before residency grabs you by the balls and won't let go for four years. What do you say?"

"Don't know how." Before he let his interest in the least bit get piqued, John had to put the truth out there.

Apparently expecting an outright no, Aaron's assurance sounded victorious. "You say yes, and let me do the rest."

While John's heart had joined with his dick in suddenly wanting this, his freaking brain popped in with, "Why?"

"Won't need to ask that after two weeks with me and the rocks."

The unexpected dip of Aaron's voice into sultriness stunned even John's stubborn brain into agreeing. "Yes," he blurted out before the more logical of his brain cells re-fired.

"Great! I'll pick you up at DIA on June seventh. Leave everything else to me." John pictured a naked Aaron bouncing on the balls of his feet. He turned to logistics to calm his imaginative cock down.

"What kind of equipment do I need?"

"You can play with my equipment, doc." John's cock attempted a back flip. "Gotta go," Aaron added, and he was gone. Just like that.

For four months John hadn't heard a peep from his pilot, but when June seventh came on a stormy Florida morning, John Castle was sitting on a plane to Denver. As the lightning lit up the Tampa Bay skies around him, John felt nervous for the first time in his adult life.

"Should have turned my ass around right then." He ducked his head and whispered into the collar of the sweater he just bought down the concourse. He was fucking freezing, sitting by the luggage claim and the big wide-open doors of the arrival bay. He didn't dare venture anywhere else, though. John was insistent on convincing himself that picking Aaron out of a crowd might prove tricky since he hadn't seen the man in four years. So, keeping an eye on the arrival door was his best bet in narrowing down his prospects—as if he wouldn't recognize the man he'd been jerking off to for months.

His palms were beginning to sweat. He dragged his hands out from under his thighs and preceded to count on his fingers the ways Fate had lately been such a bitch.

Number one was simple and needed repeating: It was snowing in June! For God's sakes, he was Floridian!

The second intentional screw-up had been the Lady sending Aaron overseas for four fucking years! Even the bitch had to admit that was extreme.

Number three he could narrow down to one word: technology. If it wasn't for the damn phone, the damn Internet, the damn United States Postal Service, then Aaron would have just faded away into a memory. But, hell no! There had to be stupid technology keeping the whole world in touch. Had he mentioned yet that she was a bitch?

Good old number four was a dastardly, ironic deed: Lady Fate had brought his stinking plane in on schedule. He had been counting on being late, having Aaron tapping his toes, gnawing his nails, all anxious and unnerved to catch that first glimpse of John. Yeah, well…

Shit, he was screwed.

"Cold?"

John nearly pissed his pants as Aaron's voice suddenly lilted down sarcastically from above and behind. He heaved himself up from his luggage perch and turned ever so casually around.

Aaron Chambers was a walking wet dream. Light blue jeans he must have been poured into covered his thighs that had swelled into the delicious realm of thundering. A black T-shirt skimmed his upper body, revealing pert nipples that were absolutely thriving in the cold. Aviator sunglasses, short brown hair bleached to a soft blond by the sun and a smile that could jumpstart a corpse completed the vision. John gruffly said, "What the hell kind of weather is this?"

Aaron cocked his head to the side and softened his smile. "It's not Afghan weather and that's all that matters to me." He swept off his glasses with an attractive ease, then proceeded to check John out from head to toe. When he reached the green eyes, he concluded with a playful smirk, "Sure good to see you, doctor."

"Captain." The sudden upturn of John's lips was really impossible to hide, especially after Aaron enveloped him in a brief but warm hug. Before Aaron pulled away, John muttered in his ear, "Thank you for not getting your head blown off."

As he stepped slowly back, Aaron's voice caught as he reminded John of his more probable fate. "Fireball."

John laughed. "Good thought. I'm freezing my balls off here."

"Wimp." Aaron snorted, like any red-blooded soldier would.

"I'm here, aren't I?"

"Point." Even Aaron couldn't deny that agreeing to this had taken if not guts than a fair leap of faith. Looking down at John's luggage and shaking his head at John's obvious inexperience at packing for adventure, Aaron asked with a wide grin, "You ready to let loose?"

"Are *you*?" John asked in complete seriousness, obvious implications attached.

Aaron could only shrug and give a crooked, though promising, flash of a smile. "Trying." Reaching down to pick up John's luggage, only to have the doctor grab it right back out of his hands, Aaron asked as they began to make their way out into the freezing parking lot, "How's Licia? I get letters, but you know…"

"She's a 16-year-old brat… and perfect." Although Liam and John were no longer sleeping together, they did run in to each other in classes. John always made a point of asking after Licia.

"Glad to hear it." Aaron smiled in relief.

John took advantage of the opportunity and asked, "On or off?" He knew Aaron would know he was talking about Rosalyn.

Aaron did and replied with another now-damp shrug, "Been off for a while."

John's silent applause was hidden behind a nonplussed, "No comment."

Aaron took the obvious lie in stride and asked with a lack of all innocence, "Been keeping yourself busy?"

"Casually"—in other words, a collection of one-offs and a calloused right hand—"when I have the time."

Aaron's grin turned smug. "And I got two weeks?"

"Point," John begrudgingly conceded.

The cocky spring to Aaron's step did not go unnoticed.

* * *

They were heading south. The canyons they were going to scale were in a little-known state park frequented mostly by fellow rock-climbing enthusiasts with a desire for small crowds and magnificent climbs. Normal travelers would have reached the park in two hours, but it would take Aaron and John four.

The interstates that grew out of Denver's city-center covered Colorado like a spider's web, taking travelers anywhere and everywhere they'd ever want to go. Aaron avoided them like they were the plague. Colorado was best seen on its county roads. Two lanes of long grey silk, on a map they were the fiber of the state's fabric. Aaron and his pick up truck clung to them gleefully as the sparsely traveled roads crossed mountain, plain and valley alike. Aaron would have whistled in utter contentment if it had disturbed the deafening chasm of silence enveloping the right side of his truck.

The drive had been simple, quiet. So quiet, in fact, that Aaron had given serious thought about taking out a barn just to force a couple of words out of John's mouth. The strong and silent type, Aaron was quickly learning, was a dandy of a myth but a boil on the butt in reality. He snickered and thought about sharing that one with the good doctor, but the sour look on the handsome face in the passenger's seat of the truck put a kibosh on that tactic.

He tapped his gloved fingers on the steering wheel as mile marker 105 crawled by.

* * *

John had to start remembering to wear looser jeans around this guy. His hard-on was killing him. He didn't want to maneuver too much in his seat and give his problem away. That was the trouble with hanging around with another man: he knew all the tricks of dealing with a misbehaving dick.

So he decided to just keep quiet, keep looking out the passenger window and keep not thinking of the man currently jerking off the gear shift.

Mile marker 153 slipped frustratingly by on a downshift.

* * *

Aaron's cell phone rang at marker 172. He answered the "unknown caller" with a quizzical lift to his brow, "Captain Chambers here."

"Told him yet?" Some voices can't be erased from memory no matter how hard time wears at them. Liam Tasker had one of those voices.

"You have got to be shitting me." Disbelief riddled Aaron's words, as he didn't quite know whether to laugh or reach for his gun. He did, however, slow the truck to a safe crawl.

"I've been waiting," the weasel singsonged.

"What the hell for?" Aaron all but yelled. Realizing his mistake, he clamped his mouth shut and took two slow, deep breaths before continuing calmly, "You know what, Liam? Never mind. You want me to tell him, I'll tell him." Turning to John, whose jaw line had transformed into a block of cold steel, Aaron lightheartedly announced to him, "I watched Liam suck you off that day in the back room. I shot my pants full of come without even laying a finger on my dick." Returning his full attention back to the phone and the scoundrel listening in, Aaron asked, "Happy?"

"Is John?"

Good question. Falling back onto his deep-breath strategy of only moments before, Aaron finally forced himself to peek over at John. What he saw shocked the hell out of him. "Well, actually, he's got this big dopey grin on his face and he's..."

John moved in quickly.

Not giving a thought to his seatbelt, John threw himself over towards Aaron and snatched the phone right out of his hand. Then, not bothering to retreat back into the lonely confines of his own seat, he growled to Liam while only inches from Aaron, "Don't fucking call again. I've got some Air Force cock to suck."

Aaron counted them very lucky that he didn't veer them off a cliff face. "Give me some warning next time, doc! Shit!" They had come to a bumpy stop at an empty overlook off the side of the main road. Aaron looked like he was having a cardiac arrest as he shoved John back, dropped his head to the steering wheel, and wheezed.

Happily, John knew the problem wasn't Aaron's heart. He slammed shut the phone, then snickered as he glanced over at the blanched man. "Did I hear a 'next time'?"

Aaron chuckled into the wheel. "If I stroke out here, feel free to do whatever you want with my body. Just send the bastard some hot pics and I'll veg away happily."

John laughed as he chunked the phone back into Aaron's lap. "How close are we to…wherever we're going?"

"Why?" Aaron raised up and tried not to look as disheveled as he felt. He wouldn't be surprised if John just wanted to bolt. "Nice joke, by the way. Think Liam got the point?" Aaron didn't blame John one iota for using him to get that creep off his back. Yep, nice joke.

John suddenly grabbed Aaron's chin, turning the pilot to look him dead in the eye, "I was serious." Letting him go as quickly as he had laid hands on him, John looked out the windshield and asked again, "So, how far?"

Aaron knew this was it. He jumped in with both feet and eyes wide open. His gaze burned a hole through the crotch of John's jeans. "Close enough to keep that monster interested."

A blush fired John's cheeks for the first time in years, giving even more heat to his words, "Trust me, with you that won't ever be a problem. If it wasn't sub-zero out there, I'd bend you over the hood of this truck and fuck your ass so hard you'd still be feeling it when you make general." He purposefully leveled his breath. "But since that's a no-go, you'd better…"

"Get going?"

"Yeah."

They got going.

Several miles flew by before John spoke again. His tone brooked no argument that he was serious. "Asking this once. And just this once. Are you sure?"

It was a loaded question. Aaron, however, knew the answer. "I want it. A lot. Might as well try it. It's not like I can't go back."

John snorted. "And you swept fair Rosalyn off her feet with that talk?"

Aaron didn't smile. "This isn't about love, John." He had to make that clear.

John never flinched, just nodded slowly. "This is about fucking. I get that. An itch you need scratched." His lips twisted up wryly as he admitted, "An itch I've been wanting to scratch since you leaned over that damned iron gate."

"Good. We're on the same page." He didn't know if he completely believed John, but he was willing to take that leap for—well, for what John was currently doing.

Having reached over into Aaron's lap, John roughly kneaded the penis and balls beneath the denim.

Aaron groaned appreciatively, curling his fingers

tighter around the steering wheel, fighting to keep his foot from driving the accelerator through the floorboard.

"Enough talking?" John asked, retrieving his hand from Aaron's lap, his *innocent* groping at a merciful end.

Biting his lower lip in simmering frustration, Aaron looked up and saw an old wooden billboard for a little motel. Proudly proclaimed across the sign in blue spray paint were the words, "Yes! We're open!"

"Happy Hills Motor Lodge okay with you?" he asked. The bastard had better say yes. It was only ten miles away and that was about all the mileage his now raging hard-on could take.

John glanced up just in time to see the billboard speed by his window. He looked under-impressed but replied in deference to his own jean-tenting, "Sure. Better than that damned white bathroom."

"Ten miles," Aaron reiterated with a grateful nod, just in case some anxious parts of his anatomy hadn't been listening. "No problem."

A couple of miles dragged by, both men trapped in silence. Finally, Aaron couldn't take the sound of his own mind any more. "Mind clueing me in on what's going on with your psycho ex?" If they were going to be fuck-buddies, might as well be blunt fuck-buddies.

John seemed a little uneasy at the question. "I guess you could say we're civil."

Aaron rolled his eyes. *"Were* civil, John." He grabbed his phone and waved it around. "This kind of crap is not civil."

Aaron thought he caught John wince at that

before he covered up with some straightforward facts. "He just doesn't like you. Liam's got a lover and has had him for years now. His guy is hot property too. Football player."

It was Aaron's turn to wince. He could just imagine how a major college football program would love to deal with an openly gay player. Life could be shit sometimes. "Hush-hush?" he guessed.

"Yeah."

Aaron took the opportunity to bring up the shit his career forced him to face. "About that…"

John cut him off with an understanding smile. "It'll be our dirty little secret."

John knew. Of course, he knew. "Don't ask, don't tell" must be a hell of a joke. Deciding to deflect attention away from the antiquated ways of his so-called *boss*, Aaron pointed out with a grin, "Not little." His gaze zeroed in quickly on John's impressive package.

"I guess you'd know," John taunted.

Aaron didn't stand down. "Not apologizing."

"You'd better not." As if taking possession of a wayward toy, John reached over and grabbed Aaron's thigh in a heated lock. "I'm looking forward to getting even."

Aaron gulped and looked hopefully down at the odometer. "Five miles," he reported hesitantly.

"Four and three quarters," John corrected with infuriating ease.

Thankfully, they pulled into the tiny parking lot only minutes later.

* * *

With a gruff "Stay here," John climbed out of the truck and went inside to check them in.

Appreciating the unspoken gesture of "sneaking in the military man," Aaron settled back in his seat and took a long look at the Happy Hills Motor Lodge. Under a canopy of pine trees, behind a light garishly blinking "Vacancy," sat the little hotel. It was made up of two buildings, both one-story affairs that sat back to back just off the roadside. In an aura of red from the cola machine inside, the office sat at one end of the front building, door propped open despite the unusually chilled weather. It looked like the place had been built in the '50s, with updates only begrudgingly made. There were only two other vehicles in the gravel parking lot; one, the receptionist; the other, he guessed, was the maid's.

John was gone longer than Aaron expected, but when he did make his way out he was jangling a key in his left hand. "Around back. Room 17." Aaron looked askance at the defunct Baltimore Colts key ring. John quickly assured, "I checked the room out. Got the place for two weeks."

"But…" Aaron sputtered.

John shrugged, making no excuses as to his reasoning, "Got 14 days with you. Not wasting any of them driving around."

"Two weeks?" That slipped out unintentionally in a squeak. Aaron was trying his hardest to play this cool, but he was as nervous as hell. He cleared his throat and tried to recover. "The whole two weeks?"

John had the balls to look smug. "Up to it, soldier?"

Aaron glanced down at his hard-on that was

currently trying to bully its way out of his jeans and found his answer. "Apparently, I am."

* * *

The room was quaint. Yellow walls that had once been airy now erred more to the side of dingy. Thick brown curtains on hundreds of tiny gold loops spanned the ceiling to air conditioner front window. Two double beds with dark green knit comforters were separated by a wooden crate on four legs that Aaron assumed was the attempt at a bedside table. No headboards, no reading lamps, no desk for the lone slatted chair to sit under. Aaron was not looking forward to the bathroom.

"Two weeks?" he asked again with skepticism ripe on his tongue. He eyed the smug John like he was a madman. "I've got a tent in the back of the truck that would put this place to shame."

"We need room." The cocky bastard undid his borrowed coat. "Central heat." He slipped it from his shoulders. "Good lighting." He let the coat fall to the floor. "Room service." He reached for his button fly. "An unlimited supply of clean sheets." He undid the top button. "And a shower to finish what I started." He undid the second button, then stopped. Looking up at Aaron's very interested face, he queried, "Any complaints?"

"I'll need to see that menu."

"Help me." John tore himself away from Aaron's sweltering gaze and headed to the box on legs. "Let's put this in that corner over there." He jerked his head to the empty space by the bathroom door.

Not quite seeing where John was going with this, Aaron nevertheless shrugged and helped John secret the table away. "What are we doing?" he finally asked as John purposefully strode to the far side of the farthest bed.

"We're doubling the double, Sherlock," was John's wise-ass response as he shoved one bed right up against the other.

A devilish smile hung on Aaron's lips as he was quickly getting the idea. "An Olympic-sized bed? You know, my expectations are skyrocketing."

John strode across the room, his brutish momentum pushing Aaron back against the wall. John did not touch him as he stood with his hands on the hips of his unbuttoned jeans. His green eyes blazed in some unknown passion; his voice was a husky dare. "I'm prepared to give you what you want." Slowly he ran his appraising gaze up and down the pilot as if Aaron were a rack of raw meat and John a starving man. "But you've got to take it. Agreed?"

Arousal coursed through Aaron's body like some hard-ass liquor that both numbed and scorched as it made its way down. It took a moment, but he finally breathed out, "Agreed."

Like a predator freshly fed, John grinned and reached out for Aaron's fly.

Shocking the hell out of John, Aaron shoved his hand away. He grabbed John by the waist of his jeans and yanked the man against him. His fingers quickly crawled down to the man's crotch, finding the remaining closed button and undoing it without bothering with consent. "You want to top?" Grabbing the waistband of John's briefs with one hand, he shoved his other hard into its treasures. What he found, he squeezed. "You're going to have to work for it." Aaron cocked his head to the side and smirked in wicked mischief. "Agreed, doctor?"

"Hell, yeah," John growled just before he devoured Aaron's mouth.

The game was on.

* * *

For five hours, the men battled.

The first strike was John's.

Grabbing either side of Aaron's head, John rammed his tongue down his throat. Sucking in Aaron's lips, he grazed their velvet soft flesh with his teeth and nibbled.

Aaron chuckled inside of John's mouth, John's tiny bites tickling his senses. This threw him off of his footing of attack and Aaron's hand relinquished its firm hold on John's shaft and balls. Like a viper, John struck with precision, speed and guile.

Curling his fingers through the short strands of Aaron's hair, he yanked him back.

Aaron lost a fraction of his balance.

John wrapped his leg around the back of Aaron's, sending the soldier falling toward the wall.

Instinctually, Aaron grabbed on to John's shirt.

John released his head, and shoved the unbalanced man hard into the yellow wall.

Aaron hit the barrier with a surprised "Oomph!" With the loss of breath came the loss of his knees. For the tiniest slit of a second, Aaron's legs began to buckle.

John stepped back, bent over, shoved his shoulder hard into Aaron's gut and hefted him into a brutal fireman's carry.

Stunned, Aaron couldn't regain his bearings until it was too late and he was being thrown back onto the joint beds. His body bounced only once before all his combat skills came rushing back to his mind's forefront.

The second strike was Aaron's.

Fisting his fingers into the cheap comforter, he gained just enough leverage to kick his shoes from his feet. Breathless, he smiled as he heard them hit the floor on either side of John's imposing figure towering at the end of the bed. With a defiant quirk to his lips, he dared rather than asked, "Rough?"

Still standing, still smirking, John toed his own shoes off. "Yeah." He kneeled on the bed, straddling the bottom half of Aaron's legs. The position was by no means tenable. It was an unspoken dare of his own.

"Careful what you wish for." Aaron kicked out his left leg and brought it up to John's crotch. With the sole of his socked foot, he began to roughly massage the denim-trapped hard-on. He grinned as John, with eyes beginning to fog, leaned closer into his machinations and moaned. Cocksure and arrogant, Aaron brazenly teased, "I always cheat."

John let his eyes drift shut as he answered in the midst of a pleasure-filled groan, "Fair enough." With fumbling fingers he reached up to the waistband of his own jeans and yanked the already loosened barrier down his thighs. His shaft swelled and masted higher in his white cotton briefs. Through a slit in his barely closed eyes, John waited until the whole of Aaron's attention rested on John's growing cock. "Because I always win."

The third strike was unexpected, fierce and devastating.

In a steel grip with both his hands, John grabbed hold of Aaron's raised ankle and wrenched the leg upside down.

With a pained grunt of startled protest, Aaron's body had no choice but to follow suit and follow his foot and ankle over. He flopped indignantly onto his stomach.

John pounced. Throwing his complete body weight atop of Aaron, he blanketed the man from head to foot.

Though trapped, Aaron tried to push himself up on his arms.

John made sure he failed. Snaking his own arm down and around Aaron's waist he shoved his hand down Aaron's pants and grabbed the man's dick and pulled.

All control left Aaron's arms and he fell again defenseless beneath John. He grunted out in rising anger, "Get. Off. Me."

John laughed snidely in his captive's ear. "Get you off? Is that what you said?" Wrapping around the other side of Aaron's squirming body, John's other arm joined his first on its assault of Aaron's trapped cock. "I can do that." John's machinations turned immediately more intimate. Every flick of his finger, every measured twist of John's wrist against Aaron's crotch was no longer meant to stun, but to wring out from every pore pure unadulterated pleasure.

As the onslaught began, John could feel every fiber of Aaron's body suddenly tense beneath his own.

Aaron threw his head back, trying to catch John on the chin.

John was ready and easily ducked the attempt. Aaron's failure allowed John better access and grip to the engorging cock. John chuckled as he now pumped mercilessly on the shaft.

"Fuuuck!" Aaron wailed from behind gritted teeth as he pounded his forehead in maddening frustration onto the mattress. All of his resisting strength was slowly leaking out of his now weeping cock. Every drop of blood in his body was rushing to his groin, leaving nothing but an electric feeling of numbness behind in each drop's wake. His whole body was catching on fire. "Fuck... fuck..." The word was no longer an exclamation of anger but a growing plea. He tried one last time to buck John off him, but the attempt was weak and doomed to failure. With a long, hard sigh, Aaron went limp under John and surrendered to the sexual onslaught.

Reveling in his victory, John dropped a kiss to the back of the sweat-drenched head. "That's better, my pet." If there was any fight left in Aaron, John knew he would have bucked at that, but Aaron just lay there, docile, soaking up every morsel of pleasure John allowed him.

John's own cock swelled. This was the power trip of John's fucking dreams.

Too bad it was over.

Although his body might be lost in a haze of lust, Aaron's mind still clung to a shred of reason and strategy. Waiting until he could sense John's ego inflate to distracting girth, Aaron grabbed John's offending wrists and rolled both men over. Scrambling to get off John's chest before John regained his bearings, Aaron regretfully yanked the magical hands carefully away and rolled until he was kneeling beside a still prostrate John.

John's eyes were as wide as saucers as he demanded, "What the fuck?"

Breathing in gasps and leftover moans, Aaron reached to his jeans and hurriedly undid them. Clumsily, he then shoved his jeans and his black briefs down to his knees. He pointed indignantly at his bobbing cock. "You are going to finish this face to fucking face. Got it?"

John threw his head back and laughed. "Yeah, I got it." Reaching over, he grabbed the pilot's arm and yanked Aaron down on top of him. Sharing breaths, he asked the man at his lips, "Better?"

"No," Aaron petulantly replied as he pushed John's underwear clear of his straining cock. Smirking, he tossed back, "Better?"

As the heads of their erect penises met skin to skin for the first time, John growled in rocketing pleasure. "Fucking bastard."

"Not yet, I'm not." Aaron began to create the most delicious friction as he rubbed his body roughly up and down against John's.

John took up the rhythm with the fervor of a wild beast.

Aaron let him roll them to their sides.

John let him rip his shirt over his head.

Aaron grabbed John's right nipple and bit.

John grabbed Aaron's left ass cheek and kneaded.

Skin on skin. Sweat on sweat. Eye to eye. The doctor and the pilot came like fucking freight trains.

* * *

John recovered first. Looking at the man he still held in his arms, he grinned like a little boy given a sparkling new toy. "Can I fuck you?"

Aaron opened bleary eyes and couldn't help but grin back. Feeling John's dick twitch against his hip, Aaron shook his head at John's fortitude. "Giving me no time to recover, doctor?"

John brushed a gentle kiss across his lips. "You're all loosened up now. It'll be easier for you, I promise."

Any qualms or hesitations vanished into thin air at the mere presence of John's vow. "Okay. Fuck me," he answered with more confidence than he felt.

"Roll over onto your stomach."

"But—"

"Trust me." John cupped Aaron's face within his hand and kissed each of Aaron's still fluttering eyelids.

Sleepily, Aaron sighed and relented, slowly rolling over.

John grinned at the half-asleep man and gently slipped him out of the rest of his clothes. He slipped out of his own as Aaron gently snored.

John lightly smacked Aaron's ass, chuckling as the man barely stirred. "I'm not fucking a corpse." He noticed a gentle rocking of Aaron's body. Grabbing Aaron's elbow he pulled the man's arm out from under him. "You little fucker, no jerking yourself off." At Aaron's unrepentant chuckle, John manhandled both his hands up to the head of the bed. "Now, keep them there, or I'll tie them down."

Aaron didn't protest.

John's cock did more than twitch. Bending down to rub his palms appreciatively over the steel curves of Aaron's ass, John gently massaged the cheeks while covertly moving Aaron's legs farther and farther apart. Aaron was spread-eagle in a matter of moments. John leaned back onto his heels to appreciate the view. "You okay?" he asked as Aaron's breaths got suspiciously long.

Aaron nodded sleepily into the sheet. "Feels good."

"Remember that feeling." John chuckled, knowing the inevitable pain that was to come. "I'll try to make this easy."

"Just drill me, doc. I can take it." Aaron's bravado overran his smarts.

John cocked his head and tried to measure Aaron's coherency. "I think you're—"

"Fuck! Me!" Aaron yelled petulantly into the mattress as he waved his ass alluringly up into the air.

Grabbing the lube from his bag on the floor, John lathed himself up and warned, "All right, big fella, you asked for it." With two fingers shining in lube, John rammed the slicked digits into the virgin ass hole.

Aaron jumped like a cattle prod had just been fired up his butt. "What the…"

With long, gentle strokes of his free hand down Aaron's now heaving back, John calmed the frightened colt. "Shhh. Just relax, and feel me fill you."

Aaron's hands fisted the sheets above his head but he didn't make another sound of complaint. His breathing hitched only a few more times before settling back into a normal rhythm.

"That's it. That's good. Just feel me touch you." John's fingers began to scissor inside him. Slowly the scissoring grew wider until a third finger was easily slipped in too.

Aaron moaned in pain, turning irrevocably into pleasure.

John watched the muscles ripple through Aaron's body as Aaron rocked slightly to the beat of his fingers. John gave him no warning as he slipped his fingers out and slipped his hard, weeping cock in.

"Ugh!" The cry into the mattress was guttural, but Aaron didn't try to pull away.

John stroked his lower back a few times before he gently lifted Aaron's hips off the bed. A pillow was quickly shoved under Aaron's pelvis to keep his ass ripe for John's picking.

John began to pump.

Aaron grunted as he began to rock back to meet the thrusts.

"That's it," John's voice hitched as he pushed in to his hilt. "Feel me fuck you." John slipped his hand under Aaron and began to gently stroke his growing hard-on.

The long moments of thrusting and stroking stretched into minutes, the minutes into nearly an hour. Both men were sweating profusely, rocking violently, cursing incessantly as their climaxes neared.

"I'm going... to come... inside you," John slowed his thrusting just enough to make the statement a question.

In response, Aaron pushed John's dick further up his ass. "Do it!"

With a deep breath, John changed the angle of his

fucking just enough to shove his cock hard into the virgin prostate.

Aaron screamed as the orgasm violently tore his world apart.

John exploded inside the spasming body.

As Aaron felt John's seed flood his ass, raw ecstasy ripped his consciousness away.

* * *

To the victor go the spoils, they say. Looking down at his come-covered body and the passed-out lump of sex beside him, John wondered what happened to the damned spoils if the battle was too close to call. Throwing his arm clumsily over his eyes, John conceded that he didn't give a fuck. He was too wiped to get up and piss, let alone deal with a wanton spoil.

John drifted on the wake of his spent endorphins for longer than he'd care to admit. Just listening to his lungs slowly regain their natural rhythm had lulled him into a shallow slumber that even his bladder couldn't disturb.

"Ow."

That little exclamation from the occupied mattress to his right was enough to pry open one of John's still fogged-up eyes. He really couldn't see much, his face still nestled into the dark crook of his arm; but he groaned at the effort just the same. When he got no sympathy from the mass at his hip, he surrendered his senses to the task of forming an appropriate question. "You okay?" he managed to slur in what he hoped would be found intelligible by a soul as thoroughly fucked as him.

The mattress moved beneath John. A breathy gasp accompanied the tiny squeak of the bed as the complaint was repeated in just as surprised of tones. "Ow?"

"Itssupposedtohurt." The words all ran together like homemade jelly on rye toast... Huh? Dragging his arm off of his face, John figured he best see for himself what kind of condition his cohort was really in.

A mile of sweat-drenched skin stretched out before John's eyes. Aaron lay sprawled on his stomach. Enticing even John's overtaxed and milked-dry libido were two of the firmest ass cheeks the Air Force had ever sculpted; they laid slightly reddened and absolutely perfect, innocently awaiting another drilling. Following the long line of spine over a back still hitching in blatant exhaustion, John found a head of mussed light brown hair rising from the mattress. He was met with big brown eyes simmering in comical accusation.

John snickered in self-satisfaction.

"Bastard." Aaron dropped his head back down to the mattress, smashing his face into the bouncy firmness.

Laughing as heartily as his sprained lungs allowed, John flopped his arm onto Aaron's back and patted him condescendingly. "You want me to kiss it and make it better?"

Aaron's head popped up in immediate though fleeting interest. His body protested the movement and its accompanying thought violently. Aaron threw John his dirtiest look before letting his head plop back down.

With a grunt and a huge amount of effort, John pushed himself up onto his elbows and looked down at the man. "You know, you're fucking gorgeous."

Aaron peeked up at John to find him smiling, but his green eyes were serious. Aaron shifted, rolling over on to his side to face him. "Thank you. You were…" His voice drifted away for a moment before returning, deeper. "I don't think there are words."

John's hand found Aaron's face and cupped it gently. "Think I could kiss you before I fuck you again?"

"Yeah," Aaron replied softly before closing his eyes and leaning in.

John kissed him for longer than he fucked him.

* * *

"Whippersnapper." The word would barely form on his lips, let alone fall from his tongue on more than a frail whisper. They had finally called John. They had finally let him see Aaron. His condition was stable, his prognosis fair. Time was what Aaron needed now, and until he woke up nobody would be able to tell John more. Now, as John stood in the doorway of the tiny ICU cubicle, all he could mutter was an idiotic nickname from a lifetime ago. A new voice broke into his foolish reverie.

"We're bending the rules for you, doctor." Instead of the garish bright colors most of the nurses were forced to wear, she was wrapped in a soft grey sweater covering simple white scrubs. She stood with her weathered hands in the long cardigan's pockets, and she slightly swayed back and forth on her nurse's shoes as she grimly guarded the scene.

"I know." He jerked his head forward in what he hoped would pass as a nod as he stumbled an awkward step toward the bed.

A strong, warm hand unexpectedly ballasted him from behind. He turned just enough to see over his shoulder steely gray eyes above a heartening smile. "So, just try to relax as much as this situation will let you. Know that you can stay as long as you want." Slowly, the hand moved in a gentle, comforting circle across his back, her earlier ice having melted completed away. "So no worries about that, all right?"

"Thank you."

The woman maneuvered her considerable weight between John and the open door. She lowered her voice only a smidgeon, a further testament to her senior position in the hospital. "And remember, this isn't a military hospital. This room is my domain." Just enough of the frost had returned to turn her words from simple chatter to effective threat. "'Loose lips sink ships,' and all that other rubbish. You got me?"

It was obvious that she got him, and Aaron. It was an unfathomable relief. "Yes," he replied simply, allowing the gratitude to show in his usually guarded eyes.

She acknowledged John in much the same manner. "Good, now I'll leave you alone. Call me for anything." She motioned briefly to the call button beside the bed, knowing further explanations were not needed when it was a doctor nested at a bedside. She moved slowly, shuffling her roundness to the door with no great speed. "By the way"—she turned and briefly smiled over her shoulder—"my name is Rose."

"You're kidding?" John asked, although he was

truthfully too numb to fully recognize all the irony that had just flooded into the room with her name.

"No." But Rose recognized the beginnings of a story when she heard one. "Why, may I ask?"

"Long story." John sighed and turned his attention back to the bed.

He had no need to see Rose to know she was offering another rare smile. "Next time I'll bring us both some of the good coffee and you can tell me a tale." The seasoned nurse in her made her add, "That is, only if you want to, doctor, of course."

John still looked only at Aaron as the words came softly. "Thanks, Rose."

The rubber soles shuffled away.

There wasn't a chair. There was only a stool with wheels. Visitors weren't meant to stay long here, only patients. Grabbing the black vinyl seat and wincing at the squeak of the wheels on the linoleum, John rolled the stool to the bedside and sat gingerly down. He didn't want to hear that squeak again. He just wanted to listen to the machines as they busily kept his lover alive.

There were beeps of every tone and urgency, and there was the warm whirring of mechanisms feeding hungrily on electricity. John closed his eyes and thanked God that they lived here and now.

Slowly, John reached out and touched the back of Aaron's hand with a coward's reverence. The skin was hot and dry, and a grayness lingered just under the surface, making the blue of his veins stand out in ghastly accord.

Anger at himself suddenly boiled up inside of John. "Damn it!" he cursed as he realized he was touching Aaron like he were dead or a stranger. He grabbed Aaron's hand with a grip the devil himself couldn't break. John leaned down and whispered in the unconscious man's ear, "I'm never letting you go. Never."

* * *

Liam Tasker knew this hospital. He knew it well. He had interned here only a year ago. He used that familiarity to his advantage.

He waited until Rose took her coffee break before making his way to the nurses' station at the ICU.

A hunched figure in the first room caught his eye.

Liam stared at John Castle and smiled.

* * *

For an hour, John sat there, not talking, not praying, just holding. A rustling in the hallway caused him to look up. Rose shuffled by the doorway with a tray of meds, heading for some other soul on the brink.

Just seeing her somehow snapped John out of his fugue, breathing life back into his vigil and, therefore, a little bit of life back into Aaron. Releasing his hold on Aaron's hand, John turned to rubbing slow circles on Aaron's forearm as he mused aloud, "What is it with you and Roses and Rosalyns?" The forced laugh came out as more of a strangled sob. He bit hard on his lower lip, tasting the warm saltiness of the blood, concentrating on the sharp pain, until he was able to carry on with more restraint, "She doesn't look much like a Ro, so I think it'll be all right."

John dropped his head to his chest and sighed. "Fair Rosalyn." He laughed sadly at the nickname, then sobered completely. A road map of roads not taken weaved its way across John's mind. Her name was on the paths of so many of them, all of them leading to destinations other than this. "The day you were killed, Rosalyn, everything in our worlds changed."

Chapter Seven

Ropes

When John Castle thought of his new home in Panama City, Florida, he thought of his toes. Honey-stained hickory floors, wire-brushed to bring out the grooves of the grain, felt divine beneath his bare feet. The serpentine lines of rough texture massaged his soles every time he padded from shower to bed, but hardwood floors weren't meant for the kitchen, or so the salesmen kept telling him. John didn't give a fuck. He wanted to stand on these floors every night in his bare feet as he scoffed down chocolate-chip ice cream with a chaser of cold milk. So at 3:20 in the afternoon of August tenth, John in his bare feet stood in his kitchen completely content with the world.

The television played in the background.

John stuck the freshly washed celery stick into the glass bowl of cream cheese and sighed happily as the cool and the crunch exploded in his mouth.

The mournful chimes of "Breaking News" drifted absently across the room.

John took a sip of iced tea as he only leant a half ear to the local reporter and her harried words. "As reported earlier this afternoon, and after receiving confirmation from Tyndall Air Force Base, we are saddened report the death of one of our local pilots. A captain, whose name is being withheld until family is notified, was leading a training exercise on base this morning and was killed when his plane erupted in fire. The cause of the fire is unknown and is being investigated. We'll have more when we know more. Stay tuned for updates."

John now sat on his honey-stained hickory floors, a broken glass of iced tea held in his trembling hand and the name "Aaron" frozen on his lips.

Two years had passed since Happy Hills Motor Lodge, two years of steamy buddy-fucks between two of the very best of friends. They both still saw other people, John other men, Aaron women, but neither man could keep his hands off his best friend for too long. Fate had played them kindly this time: Aaron had been assigned to Tyndall Air Force Base just outside of Panama City while John was completing his residency at Panama City's Bay Medical. John had bought a yellow house on the Gulf, Aaron a condo on the beach. The sex was phenomenal, frequent, and secret. They were each other's best fucks and best friends. Nothing more.

John knew that was a lie the moment his ass hit the floor.

The hell of losing his just-discovered heart lasted an interminable two minutes.

Aaron Chambers came crashing through the kitchen door. "What the fuck are you doing on the floor?" he asked as soon as he spotted John. Marching over to his miserable looking form, Aaron yanked him back to his feet and tossed the broken glass into the sink.

Shocked back into a measure of coherency, John said, "They said you were dead!"

Although John steadfastly refused to have a television set in his kitchen, he had relented to a small set on the breakfast room's corner table. Aaron complained continuously about the "miniscule" screen even though his eagle eyes could pick out a pixel at a 100 yards. It was to this little box that John pointed in total exasperation. Along its bottom was scrolling the news in big red letters: "Local Air Force captain killed in freak accident at Tyndall."

Aaron paled and grabbed onto the granite counter. For a horrible moment, John thought the pilot was going to pass out, but his worry was quickly dispelled when Aaron's face crumbled into raw fury.

"Fucking morons!" Aaron slammed his fist hard into the countertop.

"Don't!" John lurched forward to catch Aaron's hand before he punched the unforgiving granite again. He didn't give a shit about his counter, but he'd grown quite fond of every immaculate inch of Aaron's body. "What the hell do you think you're doing?" John grabbed him by the shirt collar and shouted right into Aaron's face.

He shoved John off, roaring as if his world had just been torn down its middle. "It was Rosalyn!" His voice shattered into a million multi-faceted pieces, his eyes wild and fleeing. "It was Rosalyn," he repeated in a voice just a shade above an anguished whisper. "She's the fucking captain who died. Not me."

John was stunned. While the pain of a senseless

143

loss hit him like a sledgehammer in the back, it was confusion and grief that sparred violently in John's mind. He muttered out as he looked accusingly at the television, "But they said 'he.'"

In an odd kind of desperation, Aaron laughed. "They're chauvinist cows, John. An Air Force pilot *has* to be a man, not…" The color drained from his face and disappeared into his words that only came faster and faster. "I saw her die. I saw Ro burn to death. The plane was on fire. She was screaming. There were sirens and yelling and all this horrible noise but I could hear Ro screaming. I swear I could, John. I tried to get to her. I could have gotten to her, but they wouldn't let me. There were all these hands and then I was on the ground and…I tried, John, but she kept screaming and screaming, until…"

"Aaron." John reached for him.

Aaron jerked away, and began pacing the hickory floors madly. "Goddamn it, John, it was supposed to be me! It was my training exercise to lead." Aaron pounded on his own chest. "*I* was scheduled to be in that plane. Not her. Not Ro." His breathing was speeding up, becoming haggard and strained. "But the schedules got screwed up and they sent me to a classroom. A fucking classroom, John! I didn't catch the mistake until…" Aaron turned from him, his eyes growing distant and dark as he was suddenly swept away into a replaying of the horror.

John didn't want him going there again. He lightly touched his back. "Hey…"

In a roar of fury, Aaron sent his fist through John's kitchen wall. Again. And again.

John tackled him from behind. They fell hard

against the broken wall, but John wouldn't let Aaron loose from the steel grasp he held him in from behind.

"Get. Off." He elbowed John hard in the gut and tried again to jerk away.

John brought them roughly down to the floor. He hissed in Aaron's ear, "I am not going to allow you to hurt yourself. Do you hear me?"

"Allow?" Aaron choked out in a harsh laugh. "This is not sex, doctor. This is life. My life. And I'll do what I damned well please."

"You did not kill her," He tried to maintain hold on the bucking man. "It was not your fault. Do you hear me?"

"Fuck you!" Aaron kicked in a cabinet door with his flailing leg.

"Hold still!"

"No!"

Somehow still retaining his grasp on the wildly struggling man, John reached down to the waist of his own khakis and yanked off his brown leather belt. Biting down on the soft curve of Aaron's neck just hard enough to momentarily stun him, John wrapped the belt around Aaron's pinned wrists and pulled the leather strip painfully tight.

Aaron yanked at the bindings, outraged, "What the hell…"

John pushed the soldier over onto his stomach, anchoring him down to the floor with a knee pushed into his lower back. John was out of breath himself and angrier than he had the right. "I told you I'm not going to let you hurt yourself. You may be a pain in the butt, but I love you." He blurted it out in heat and honesty, but immediately chickened out and lightened the weight of his accidental proclamation with sarcasm. "You know, best friends and all that shit."

Aaron, however, wasn't listening; he was simply lost. Dropping his head to the wood floor, Aaron confessed in shame, "I just want to hurt, John. I need to hurt. The pain inside is too much. Please." He was shaking, his voice choking back more emotions than his mind could handle.

John suspected what he needed, but Aaron had to say it. John laid a comforting hand on his back, leaning down to whisper, "What do you want?"

"I don't know," Aaron replied tiredly. "I have no fucking idea."

"I do." John feigned confidence although he was scared shitless. "Do you still trust me?"

"Yeah." Aaron snorted as he turned his face toward John. "About the only thing I do trust right now is you."

Carefully, John rose up and helped Aaron into a sitting position. Aaron's hands remained bound. John gently grasped Aaron's chin, forcing him to look John in the eye. "I can give you the pain, Aaron, but I won't hurt you." John looked pointedly at the hole in his kitchen wall and the cabinet door now off its hinges. "But not like that. Do you understand?"

"I don't know..." The brown in Aaron's eyes swirled in misery.

John kissed the trembling lips with a confidence that was now steadily growing. "Do you want to try?"

Aaron slowly nodded and whispered, "Yeah."

"If it gets too much or you just want to stop, you say 'whippersnapper,' okay?"

Aaron just stared at him.

John rolled his eyes. "It's your safe word, you dope." He needed a word Aaron could easily remember but a word that would not come up in normal conversation. Whippersnapper was perfect.

A sliver of a smile cut across Aaron's mouth before disappearing again into pain. "It hurts, John. I loved her. I didn't know how much until…"

John knew exactly what he meant. He hadn't known how much he loved this man until just a few moments ago when a reporter's voice briefly stole his life away. Running his thumb gently along the curves of Aaron's face, he whispered, "Come with me."

John stood up, and Aaron followed.

* * *

Floor-to-ceiling windows behind wide plantation blinds lit the guest room's pale blue walls. A lush ivory carpet matched seamlessly the plush bed linens and the cloth-covered shades of the bedside lamps. Mirrors in white wooden frames filled the walls, reflecting a hundred times over the turquoise tiled lap pool that so invitingly lay right outside the room's windows. A four-poster bed John's aunt had left him when she died filled the room with its mahogany columns and intricately carved headboard. The bed had been in storage for years, John never having the need or the room for it. Glancing again at its massive frame, John nodded in satisfaction. Finally, the bed seemed to have found a home and a purpose.

With a hand firmly on his chest, John stopped Aaron in the guest room's doorway. He looked the emotionally ravaged man straight in the face and warned gently, "When we're in there, in this room, it's different between us. It's got to be for this to work."

Aaron's exhaustion was reflected in his answer. "Yeah." He shrugged and tried to push by him into the room.

John grabbed him by the shoulders, his grasp tight and demanding of attention. "No! Not just 'yeah.'" He had to make Aaron understand that this was not just a game. If they were going to do this, they had to take it seriously. There had to be rules and an escape clause. "Remember, one word, your safe word, and we're back out here. Back to normal. Back to this." He gave Aaron the gentlest of kisses. Pulling back, he begged Aaron to understand. "One word, you got it?"

Startled by John's intensity, Aaron took a deep breath, seeming to center himself for a moment before promising with utter sincerity, "I get it, John. I do."

John believed him. He stood aside, leaving the doorway clear, and said simply, "Your choice."

Aaron walked in the door.

* * *

Only two steps into the room, John took complete control. Striding past the slowly moving Aaron, John closed the blinds and turned on every light in the room. He wanted the light to be steady, to be clear; he needed to see perfectly everything he was about to do. He tossed the pillows off the bed and stripped off the quilt and top sheet. The one fitted sheet was all the cushioning Aaron would need. Standing back, he eyed the canvas he had just created and nodded when all met with his approval. There was only one key object left to address. With confident strides, John moved behind Aaron and undid the bindings that still held his wrists together.

Absently rubbing the marks left by the belt, Aaron expressed his confusion, "I thought you were going to…"

John was suddenly right in front of him, his forefinger lying firmly over Aaron's lips. The message was clear. No talking. Aaron nodded.

Removing his finger, John took a step back and demanded simply, "Take your clothes off."

* * *

Aaron began to shake his head; he wasn't here for a fuck.

John just raised his hand.

Aaron's mouth shut tight.

John allowed a smile to curl his lips, as he explained bluntly. "Do what I say. And don't talk unless I tell you to." He waited for Aaron's nod before directing again, "Strip."

While Aaron was far from shy with his body, he wasn't an exhibitionist either. During sex, being buck naked was one thing, but this—

"I'm waiting." The reminder was not kind.

Gritting his teeth to keep from saying something stupid, Aaron quickly removed every stitch of his clothing. He silently cursed the constant tremble in his hands. Once naked, his clothes folded neatly on the floor, he looked up to find that John hadn't moved. He still stood there, arms crossed sternly across his chest, no amusement on his lips, no light in his eyes. He just stood staring at Aaron's nudity with no hint of approval or interest anywhere on his unsmiling face.

Aaron felt suddenly cold.

"On the bed." John did not allow him even time to shiver. "On your knees. Face the headboard."

Anything would be better than just standing there like some kind of naked fool, so Aaron climbed up on the sheeted bed and knelt as instructed. His heart thundered in his chest.

"Good," John commended before heading into the closet and retrieving a handful of silk ties. Tossing what Aaron knew would be his bindings at his feet, John coolly directed, "Bend over. Ass in the air. Hands to each post."

Aaron's heart leapt into his throat, and damn it if his cock didn't just twitch. Unsure, unsteady, but obedient, Aaron Chambers bent over, spread his arms up and to the side and presented his bare ass to John Castle.

His wrists were quickly and tightly bound to the corner posts. Aaron pulled on the ties once, just enough to convince himself of the tightness of the knots.

"Knees apart." A firm tapping to Aaron's inner thighs assured the desired position was acquired. Finally, John was satisfied, but warned just the same, "I will tie these thighs in place if you move an inch." The authority alone in John's voice made Aaron's thighs tremble as they struggled to hold the commanded position.

With his forehead down on the mattress, Aaron couldn't see much past the single white sheet on which he knelt. He heard a drawer open by the bed's side. Moments later, an ice-cold oil was slapped on his ass. Aaron jerked away with an indignant yelp.

John grabbed the pilot's wayward hips and sternly placed them back in their proper position. More oil was then slapped on the skin. "Oiling you down will make the sting sharper."

"Great," Aaron mumbled without thought.

Immediately, John reached between Aaron's thighs, grabbed the man's balls and sharply tugged them down once. "Silence." The one-word admonition came without emotion.

Aaron bit down hard on his bottom lip but didn't murmur another word as the oil was clinically applied.

More drawers opened and closed before he felt a shoestring being tied around his left big toe. A sharp tug assured the tie was tight but not blood-constricting. The other end of the shoelace was then similarly knotted around his right toe. The result was the toes were forced to point inward toward each other. John was kind enough to explain, "Tied like this you can't clench your ass cheeks when I hit you."

By now, Aaron was accepting of almost anything.

"I'm going to blindfold you," John informed him coldly as a sleep mask was suddenly placed over Aaron's eyes and tied tightly around the back of his head.

The darkness took him so quickly Aaron panicked and began to plea, "But…"

Two sharp jerks to Aaron's balls. "Don't make me gag you." John hissed in his ear. "You wouldn't like it, and neither would I."

Aaron had the distinct feeling that John's wants

were now paramount to his own. But Aaron was tired and hurting and he just needed someone to take control for a while, so he merely nodded and accepted the conditions.

Perhaps as a reward, perhaps just for John's amusement, John wet a finger and ran it slowly down Aaron's spine from hairline to ass. Aaron's skin erupted in tiny chill bumps, and he shivered.

"You may beg." Without further warning, the punishment began.

First, there was spanking. With his fingers splayed wide apart, John hit Aaron's left cheek with enough force to send him rocking toward the headboard.

A gargled gasp was muffled into the mattress.

Next, the right cheek.

Left cheek.

Right.

Although Aaron quickly learned to expect each slap, the sharpness and sting of the vicious smack was enough to bring tears to his eyes. After that initial gasp, however, he didn't make another sound and didn't move one inch. To his amazement, his dick even began to fill.

John smiled as he reached for the leather belt.

* * *

Wrapping the buckle end of the belt around his hand several times, John was left with a good foot and a half of smooth leather with which to work. The doctor worked expertly.

The signature sound of leather on skin resounded

through the room before the new pain reached Aaron's mind. The delayed reaction was as delightful to watch as it was brutal to bear.

Caught completely unaware, Aaron screeched.

John hit him again.

Again.

Again.

It wasn't long until the flogging produced the desired result: Aaron was crying and begging John to hit him harder.

John did as he was asked.

* * *

It was as if the pain had a life and mind of its own. It swept through Aaron's body, eating every nerve, devouring every thought. The pain literally possessed him and all Aaron wanted was more.

"Please... please, harder. Harder!" Aaron didn't care that he was crying, that he was bawling and begging. Aaron didn't care, didn't know anything but the pain—a pain different than the loss of Ro. A pain just as razor sharp but without the heart-wrenching guilt.

Shoving his ass farther up into the air, he met each strike with a masochism he'd never known before. Though this experience was not meant to be sexual, his body was reacting to it as it was. His throbbing hard-on became another element in the barrage of his senses. "Hit me! Hit me!" he pleaded as tears soaked the blindfold and his nails clawed into the posts. He just wanted, he needed more—

John stopped. The leather belt he unwound from his hand and let drop to the floor.

"What…" Aaron tugged at his bindings as he tried to turn his blinded eyes back to John. "Don't stop. Please, John. Don't." He sounded desperate. He was desperate. He didn't want the thoughts of Ro to come back. He needed that different pain. He needed that release. "What did I do wrong? Tell me and I'll fix it. I swear I'll do whatever you want."

The bed moved beneath him as he could feel the heat of John's body now beside him. A gentle hand ran gentle fingers through his sweat-soaked hair. John's words came softly, "I want you to cry for her, now. For fair Rosalyn."

The simple request broke Aaron. Tipping over on his side, he curled in upon himself as much as the binds would allow, and wept. He wept for the girl he loved. He wept for the girl he didn't love enough. He wept for what was and for what would never be. The engorged cock lay forgotten in his grief.

John carefully undid the ties and slipped the sleep mask off of Aaron's eyes. He then lay down beside him and drew his best friend safely into his arms.

* * *

Hours later, when sleep had claimed John, Aaron lay wide awake. His body ached, his heart ached, and when he closed his eyes all he could see was fire.

Blessedly, however, the anger was now gone. The dam of fury that had threatened to strangle him had crumbled beneath John's hand and John's belt. Aaron didn't understand it. Hell, he didn't even know if he liked it, but he did know it had helped—that it had perhaps, just a little, even saved him.

He loved John for that. For a lot of things, really.

Aaron snuggled back into John's arms. He didn't sleep, but he did manage to smile.

* * *

John really didn't want to have to drag Charles Dickens into this, but the man just gave him no choice. John couldn't remember the exact words, just the sentiment. Something along the lines of the crappiest of times also being the happiest of times. "That's crap," he distinctly remembered informing his tenth-grade British literature teacher. Watching the scene lazily playing out before his eyes, John wondered if he could look the woman up after all these years and give the poor woman a big sloppy kiss on the cheek in abject apology. Or maybe he would just give Mr. Dickens another shot. That is, right after he thoroughly fucked that naked ass curled up in front of him.

Deciding to stand there for just a few minutes more and enjoy the outstanding view currently sleeping in the middle of his king-sized bed, the parts of John's brain not directly associated with sex kept flashing back over to Dickens and his cockeyed words. The happiest part of his so-called phrase of the day was clearly Aaron Chambers in that sky-blue knit shirt and nothing else. Literally. He would have chuckled at his little pun but the curve of that sweet ass as it rose from the clingy confines of John's favorite shirt tucked any thoughts of snickering into the far back reaches of his mind.

John's mouth watered just looking at that body. Aaron was curled up on top of the quilted, snow-white down comforter he'd given John for his last birthday.

155

He lay oblivious to the world, with his back to the door and John eagerly leering in its frame. He wore only the shirt with his left arm tucked up under the pillow that cushioned his still-drying hair. Vestiges of his shower laid strewn about the room: his dark blue robe lying across the chair, the towel he liked to dry his hair with dropped haphazardly on the window seat, and the wet footprints drying on John's wooden floor. He must have begun to dress when Aaron's old enemy Sleep sneaked up behind John's soldier and silently took him out. At least the fiend had allowed him a bed. John would have to pass the Sleep guy a $20 for leaving Aaron in such a delectable position. The long, richly defined lines of Aaron's left leg were kicked out from the self-hug position he so often chose in sleep. With an arm curled around his chest, his chin tucked into his collarbone, his right leg acted as a beautiful balance as it lay bent at the knee on top of its outstretched counterpart. Aaron sighed in his sleep and John watched his right toes curl up and ever so slowly release.

Yes, this definitely would be defined as one of John's happiest moments.

The "crappiest" part John chose to leave acknowledged but not revisited at the moment. There would be time for those tragedies after John nibbled on those toes.

"Don't even think about it." The muffled warning seemed to crawl right out of the down of the pillow, since Aaron didn't move, not so much as a toe-twitch.

"You're supposed to be sleeping."

"I was sleeping. Toe radar." He wiggled the ten innocents mercilessly.

"Flirt."

"Perv."

Still Aaron hadn't moved; even his breathing remained deep and softly measured. John suspected it was a special ops thing. A tingle tickled up his spine.

"Stop it." The pillow moved right before Aaron's brown eyes peeked over the blue threads covering his shoulder. "Can't a guy just sleep?"

"Dick radar?" John surmised.

"Doc radar."

John laughed and finally pushed himself out of the doorway and into the bedroom he liked to call *theirs*. It warmed him knowing that after everything they had just experienced together, Aaron had returned to this room to finally surrender to sleep.

John sat down on the edge of the bed, his fingertips softly grazing the strips of brightly reddened skin. He had meant to treat these with baby oil after their session but other considerations proved to be more pressing. "These still hurt?" he asked with a wince of gentle sympathy.

Aaron rolled the upper half of his body over, allowing him a better view of his lover while still letting the air alone caress his ass. "Not bad," he answered with a bit of a shrug. He chuckled as he admitted, "Better than, well, all that stuff before."

"I'm sorry." John misunderstood and drew back.

"No!" Aaron grabbed John's wrist and brought it back to rest on his hip. "All my stuff before." He struggled for the words to say. "This helped. You helped."

"I'm glad." John choked back a wave of absurd relief. This whole affair was getting too emotional, too meaningful, for him to simply ignore.

Reaching up and tapping the wrinkles that marred John's thoughtful face, Aaron asked, "What's going on up there?"

John rubbed his hands roughly across his face, sighing into his palms. He didn't know what to say or how to say it; he just knew what he wanted. "You gave me a lot today…"

"No, I didn't." Aaron tried to sit up.

"Shh." John pushed him back down. "You gave me a chunk of yourself, in here." John tapped Aaron's head, then let his hand fall slowly away. He sounded almost sheepish as he admitted in words so soft they sounded foreign in his own ears, "I want to give you something in return."

Aaron's brows drew slowly together, his face a portrait of gentle confusion. "I don't understand."

In a cursed flurry of nerves, John blurted out, "I want you to top me."

"What?" Flabbergasted would be the simplest way to describe Aaron's response.

But John already felt awkward enough, he didn't need Aaron suddenly playing the ingénue. He snapped, "I'm giving you my virginity, so to speak. Take it or leave it, flyboy."

"You're serious?" It was obvious Aaron was. John doubted the man's eyes had ever been browner.

John felt like a heel. "Yeah." After all, it was really as simple as that.

"But—"

John dropped his head and sighed. He should have known the S.O.B. would make him spell it out. "You're my fucking best friend. Literally. I trust you with my ass, that's it."

The cat who ate the canary had nothing on Aaron's sudden smugness. He asked simply, "When?"

John closed his eyes, knowing there was no going back from this decision. All he could manage was a lowly whisper. "Now."

Aaron slowly lifted off the blue shirt. He laid John down. And with the gentleness only love can bear, Aaron Chambers took John Castle.

* * *

So many years later and that night still brought color to John's face and warmth to his heart. The experience had been exquisite, beautiful, fulfilling in every imaginable way. He had never been loved so perfectly before. It was still rare for them to switch, their psyches so attuned to their chosen roles in bed, but on occasion, beneath just the right sliver of moonlight, Aaron would take control and love John like no other.

For all the wonder that night had wrought, however, it had all begun with the tragic loss of an incredible soul. For that reason alone, John would carry fair Rosalyn in his heart always.

John ran his fingers through Aaron's hair and admitted with a self-conscious laugh, "You know, I never got that hole in my kitchen fixed. Just put that lousy calendar over the stupid thing."

"Bet he knows that," Rose commented from the doorway. In a move to soothe the newest worry lines carving chasms across that young face, she confessed as she walked in, "I didn't hear anything but that last part." She laid the palm of her hand across Aaron's forehead. "As cool as the other side of the pillow. The doctor says your friend's making great strides. Wouldn't surprise me if he wakes up soon." She bent down and laid a soft kiss to Aaron's brow. "Wouldn't surprise me if he's hearing everything we're saying."

John chuckled sadly. "He is a sneaky bastard."

"The cops know who did this?" It was the first time Rose had brought up the criminal side to Aaron's current condition. John understood very well the certain distance that must be kept between patient and practitioner and didn't begrudge the nurse her belated interest.

"Yeah," John retreated back to the metal stool and scrubbed his face roughly, trying desperately to keep himself functional. "They've got a good idea."

"You saw?" There was a softening to her skin that just hinted at paling. It was obvious the woman wanted the answer to be no. Who would ever wish a man to see his lover shot down in cold blood?

"No." John was right, she brightened.

Too bad, she wasn't the only one.

"Thank God." Liam Tasker stood in the doorway, curled around a sarcastic smile.

Chapter Eight

Chains

The hatred that had sat in John's gut like a rock for days suddenly grew flame and exploded.

John shot up, sending the metal stool he'd been sitting on crashing into a nearby machine. Alarms began to wail.

Rose moved quickly to protect Aaron.

John moved quickly to kill Liam.

Security moved quicker than all.

* * *

The snow fell on Chicago with a determined mind to meddle. Public transportation was either down or delayed to the point of sheer uselessness. The roads courted snow plows alone. The sidewalks courted no one at all.

Twenty-four floors above the city, Aaron Chambers stood at the hotel window and sulked.

John Castle sipped his cappuccino and grinned. They had checked into the plush downtown hotel last night. For the sake of Aaron's career, they had gotten two rooms, but John's had the better view so by unspoken agreement Aaron had immediately moved in. John thought the weekend was going perfectly. Aaron thought otherwise.

"Keep up that smiling and I'll ram that slipper down your fucking throat...and I use that term 'fucking throat' only figuratively, of course, since."—Aaron made a grand sweeping gesture at the winter wonderland—"this frozen, fluffy shit decided to barge in on our weekend."

"Patience, grasshopper." John lazily re-crossed his pajama-clad legs, flicking the terrycloth slippers on his feet just to piss Aaron off. There were many reasons, some real and some imaginary, for Aaron to be peeved. John enjoyed being a reason.

"I hate snow," Aaron announced to the world at large as he flopped down on the black leather sofa. He, too, was still in his pajamas but had foregone the slippers for thick wooly socks.

"No, you don't," John reminded his lover as he casually glanced at the time.

"Well, I do now." Aaron rearranged his position on the couch so that now he was sitting cross-legged, arms folded, miffed, across his chest. He looked more like a child than he probably did when he was 11. "I was thinking that you must have screwed Mother Nature over in a previous life. Let's review the facts, shall we?" He counted off the accusations with a raised finger each. "Let's see... the tornado on the night we met. The June snow on our so-called 'first date.' And now a fucking blizzard today! Of all days, John. Today!" He threw his head back, letting it hit the back cushion of the couch quite dramatically. The following sigh put the head-flop to shame. "For pity's sake, just kiss and make up with Ma Nature so I can get fucked sometime in this century."

John chuckled and sipped. He had been planning this weekend for months, keeping Aaron in the dark as to the details. The only thing John requested, other than Aaron's presence, was that he abstained for one week prior to their adventure. Aaron had put up a hell of a fight, but in the end let his curiosity win out.

"I don't know what you're giggling about." Aaron had perfected the casting of the *evil eye* the last seven days. John just caught a wallop of one. "You know, you're not getting any until I do, old man."

John knew Aaron's tricks. "You're not picking a fight or a fucking with me, so just be quiet and stew in all those pent-up juices of yours." He waved him off and reached for the business section of the paper.

"I hate you," Aaron declared.

"I know you do, dear." John threw him a kiss.

There was a knock on the door.

John carefully folded the paper, set it neatly on the table and rose slowly from his chair. A smirk of pure devilry rode his lips as he announced, "Slave-house rules, flyboy."

"What?" Aaron leapt from the couch, excitement, confusion, and a touch of apprehension warring for his reins. He, of course, knew what "slave-house rules" meant, but he could never have guessed they would be enacted here, in the hotel room.

"Just call it room service." John walked over to him, a question of consent in his eyes.

Aaron nodded.

John reached into his pocket, pulled out his

wallet, and took a gold chain out of the money sleeve. With masterful deliberation, he placed the choker around Aaron's neck and fastened the tiny links tight across the skin. Steel weaved its way through every fiber of John's countenance as the doctor demanded in an ominously flat tone, "Kneel."

Aaron dropped like a rock to his knees.

* * *

He was naked and chained before he was allowed to speak—speak being a relative term as his whole allowed vocabulary were four words: yes, no, sir, and whippersnapper. Aaron blushed to his balls when John chose that as his safe word. Revenge would be sweet, most likely involving chocolate sauce and candy sprinkles.

Drawn back to the present by a swat on his ass by the stranger he had dubbed the "bearded one," Aaron easily fell back on his years of military training and barked out an impressive, "Sir, yes, sir!"

Aaron stood in a perfect "at ease" position in the middle of the hotel room, although the iron chains and cuffs at his ankles and wrists were a new twist to the military's version. He was surprisingly calm in this first playtime with a stranger. He had suspected all along that so-called "public play" had been the intent of this long weekend, so far away from anyone they'd ever known. He'd just expected the encounter would in fact occur somewhere actually public, like a private club or dungeon. This change of plans should have thrown him completely off stride, but he was finding himself amazingly relaxed around the older gentleman and his immaculately trimmed beard. He really did wish they'd tell him the man's name.

"He's stunning," the stranger pronounced with a dazzling smile. "Lucky man, you are." He offered his hand in approval to John.

"Thank you." John preened.

Aaron added whipped cream to the planned sweet revenge.

"Does he imbibe?"

"Like a tank."

Aaron didn't think that was called for. Nuts. Spiced pecans, he thought, would go nicely with the chocolate.

"Has he agreed?"

John took out his wallet again, brought out a piece of paper. "He signed the contract."

Yes, Aaron had signed what he liked to call the "permission slip." Once they had started to seriously explore all the aspects of BDSM, they had both signed agreements as to expectations and limitations. It was very adult of them, and Aaron still liked to make digs at John's overt responsibility.

"Excellent." The bearded one gave the contract back to John. "Shall we begin?"

"Ask Aaron." It was the one and only time during the weekend that Aaron was addressed by his given name. It was the only time he felt truly uncomfortable naked in front of the stranger.

"Shall we?" the man with the whiskers asked him with a smile.

"Yes," Aaron answered dropping the "sir" as it only seemed appropriate to do.

The stranger turned back to John, and never

looked Aaron again in the eye. "What is his liquor of choice?"

Aaron had to fight hard to hold back the smile. He was definitely liking the turn this experience was taking.

"Brandy," John answered as he took out of a drawer an unopened bottle of Aaron's favorite. "A quarter of this should do."

Aaron's brow frowned. John knew he could down a good half a bottle.

Seeing Aaron's consternation, John added a few words to the stranger. "Just enough to relax him, not enough to truly cloud his thoughts."

"Of course," the bearded one answered. "It is not necessary to use such aid at all."

"I know." That was all John said and the subject of alternatives was dropped.

The stranger looked pleased, proud at John's firmness of decision. "Calm him while I prepare the room." The unknown man walked into the side room which held the king-sized bed. He shut the door behind him, for which Aaron was grateful. A tenseness he had not known existed abandoned his shoulders and slid off his body like melting ice cream.

"Good boy," John praised with a tender nod. The bottle of brandy took up the next few minutes of the doctor's attention. Once finally opened and tasted first by John, the bottle was held up to Aaron's lips and the instruction given, "Long, slow sips. Feel the alcohol melt its way through your body."

Aaron obeyed. While he had drunk brandy many times before, it had always been from a snifter. The large curve of the glass captured the aroma of the drink, easing a soul into its possession one sense at a time. Drinking from the bottle gifted no such ease.

It was happening much faster than Aaron expected. The sips that had come in quick-paced succession at the beginning now slowed to an uncalculated crawl. Just like John said, the brandy was melting everything away.

He swayed and the bottle was quickly removed. Though his thoughts were still clear, they were slower in coming. He teetered on the brink of a buzz.

John observed him closely, offering no hand to aid in his balance. "You still with me?"

Aaron worked hard to open the eyes he hadn't realized he'd closed. He stared at John for a moment while he processed the question. When he found in his mind the answer, the words surprised him by still coming out clear. "Still here. Just a little slower, sir."

John's interest seemed piqued by the use of the "sir."

Oh yeah, Aaron had forgotten. He hardly ever called John "sir," told him it reminded him too much of work. "One point to the brandy." He snickered.

John hadn't noticed, as he had moved to the bedroom's door and was talking again to the bearded stranger. "I think he's perfect."

Nice of John to say, Aaron thought as he gently swayed.

"Can you lift him?" the stranger asked.

"Yes," John answered confidently.

"Unchain him, then over the shoulder to the bed," The bearded one instructed, then disappeared back into the room.

John did as told and Aaron soon found himself

free but draped across John's collarbone. The carpet moved slowly beneath him.

The bed was a pleasant surprise. He had half thought a bed of nails would be awaiting him. The stranger, after all, did bear a striking resemblance to Bela Lugosi—with a beard. He caught this snicker before it reached his face.

Or so he thought.

"That is a sign." The stranger's voice drifted softly through the candlelit room. "If he laughs, he has topped."

Topped? He began to shake his head. He was the catcher in this relationship.

Strong hands on either side of his head stopped his gesture of denial.

Aaron looked up to find John looking down at a weird angle. A ripple of muscle beneath the back of his head finally clued him in that he was lying across John's lap. Aaron sighed, deciding to enjoy his pillow instead of worrying about who was topping whom.

Familiar fingers began to weave their way through Aaron's short hair. From front to back, they gently tingled over his scalp. It was enough to lull him asleep, if only John would let him.

"Are you listening?" John asked with a tender cadence that danced nicely with the stroking of his hair. "I want you to keep your eyes open for me. Keep looking at me. Keep concentrating on everything I'm doing to you."

It took a wavering minute to lock onto John's gaze, but Aaron did and vowed to himself that he would not look away.

"Do you feel my fingers through your hair? Do

you feel my breath brush your face? Do you feel my words enter you?"

John was talking slower now, firmer and easier for Aaron's mind to follow. "Yessir," Aaron thought he slurred, even though he knew he hadn't drank enough brandy for that. Just a trick of his mind, he guessed.

"Good. That's good."

Aaron imagined he smiled.

"Keep seeing only me. Keep hearing only me. Keep feeling only me. There is nothing in this world but me."

Aaron wanted to argue but couldn't think of a damn thing other than John. "Yessir," he tried to say again.

"Good boy."

There was a vague, distant tingling in his groin at those words, but that, too, soon disappeared behind the world that was John.

"You're melting away. You're melting into me, becoming only a part of me. An extension, pet. An extension of your Master. Your legs are my legs now. Your arms are my arms. Your cock is mine. Your mind doesn't exist beyond mine."

"Yeshirr," Aaron gargled out.

"Down, down you are falling, my pet. Down where only I can reach you. Where only I can hear you. Where only I exist."

Aaron unconsciously twitched, bracing his body for the fall.

"Even now you are falling. And with every foot that you drop, a piece of yourself drops away. Down, down, down, until you have no legs. Down, down, until you have no chest. Down until all that's left is a tiny speck of your mind. A fragile speck that I hold in my hands. A fragile speck that will disappear all together with one gentle blow of my breath."

Aaron couldn't see right anymore. He couldn't hear right anymore. He couldn't do anything anymore. He was just a speck, awaiting his Master's breath.

John softly blew across his face, and even the speck was no more.

* * *

John swore he'd never steal another breath from this earth if just a speck of Aaron would come back to him. He laughed at the irony of the world.

From across the boardroom table, Liam looked up at him and smiled. "I've missed that laugh, you know."

Although a picture of sartorial splendor in a designer three-piece black suit, white dress shirt, and a red silk tie, John couldn't believe he'd ever stuck his dick into that. "Shut up," John warned. It was all he could do not to jump over the table and rip the rat's tongue out of his throat.

The hospital security staff had proved more efficient than their polyester uniforms suggested. John hadn't landed a single blow before he was being pulled off Liam. Despite his ex's smug smile at rescue, John still took comfort in the ugly red finger marks that circled Liam's neck. Went well with his tie.

The security guards had forced both men into an empty conference room to await the police. To John's utter consternation, even when the police did arrive, there was still more waiting to be done.

John was getting damned tired of waiting, just like that day so many years ago in Chicago…

* * *

"Patience, young one," the bearded man admonished gently as he stood by John's side, a restraining hand firmly on the doctor's shoulder. Aaron lay on John's lap, with a half-lidded gaze and a breathing pattern slow and measured. Not a muscle twitched in the naked body.

"Most likely, he will hear only you," the older man advised. He looked down at the scene with approval. "He is in subspace now, a place of great fragility, a place of absolute trust."

"What do I do now?" John asked in a voice betraying his escalating nerves. For months he had studied the phenomenon known as subspace. For months, unbeknownst to Aaron, he had corresponded with the man known simply as the master of the field. That man, who lived in total anonymity, stood now by John's side.

"As I have instructed you before, you lead him. Wherever you desire him to go, he will follow." The hand disappeared from John's shoulder as the bearded man's voice moved to the far corner of the room. "His senses are heightened. Raw, one might say. His entire existence has now been pinpointed to you. It is a great honor he has bestowed upon you. Treasure it. Protect it. Nourish it and it will grow."

"How?" The affection he felt flowing from Aaron's eyes into his own was so great that John was terrified he'd surely lose it. He felt dwarfed by the enormity of Aaron's love. "I don't deserve this. Nobody deserves this."

"At this moment in time, you alone are his world. You can make his dreams come true. Make them true, young John, and yours will follow."

* * *

Despite the words sounding as if they'd come freshly sprouted from a monk on a misty mountaintop, John had taken their meaning to heart. Now, those same silly words resounded resolutely through his soul. At one moment they were a damnation of John's utter failure, at the next an anthem for the future.

If only John was allowed a future with…

"L-I-A-M. Didn't Johnny boy spell it out for you?" Liam was talking again.

The police detective had returned a few minutes ago. She was finishing the last of her paperwork before revealing to all what she'd learned in her absence.

John was giving her five more minutes before he was going back to Aaron's side, no matter who he had to plow through to get there. Although Rose had promised to stay with Aaron and let John know if there was any change, John wouldn't feel comfortable until Aaron was again in his sight. He'd let the cops deal with Liam and his lies.

The police detective cleared her throat as she finally clicked her pen closed. "We're still waiting on word about his alibi." She tossed the folder of papers across the tabletop to John. "Everything looks legit so far, though."

John glanced through the file, already guessing what he'd find. No gunshot residue on Liam's hands or clothes. No registered weapons in his name. No proof that he had ever fired a gun in his life, let alone make two pinpoint shots in the dark. Nothing but glowing reports filled his impressive work record in Pensacola—and the gold ring on his finger wasn't a fake after all.

"My wife is going to be terribly miffed that you didn't believe in her existence." Liam produced a perfectly charming chuckle at John's apparent foolishness. "She's just a person, John, not some storybook fairy. She exists whether you believe or not."

Liam being bi was a twist John hadn't expected and one he still wasn't sure he quite trusted.

The detective read the skepticism easily on John's face. "I talked to her myself, Dr. Castle. Real nice woman, real upset about her husband being accused by you." She sounded almost sorry that the news she had to give the distraught man wasn't more to his liking. "We're checking all the angles here, Doctor, but I got to say it doesn't look good."

Liam smiled sweetly.

John suddenly had a terrible feeling he'd been wrong all along.

* * *

Consciousness was unfurling around Aaron like a musty, old flag. Tattered and shot full of holes, he fought the desire to sneeze.

Fingers laced through his hair, and tugged firmly

at his strands. So firmly, it damned well hurt. Returning to the analogy his drugged-out mind thought was so clever, it was as if a heavy hand—a hand that smelled of tuna fish, was ironing out each fold of the flag. He scrunched up his nose, knowing that couldn't be right.

An unfamiliar hand grabbed his chin and shook. "Did you see? Did you see?" someone was needling into his ear.

Of course he didn't see. He didn't even have his eyes open yet. He tried to pull his chin away from the idiot with the fingers.

An open hand slapped his face.

His eyes shot open and a man with a beard suddenly filled his world.

* * *

John was beginning to panic. He had been so sure that Liam was the shooter. Finding out that he wasn't was simply incomprehensible. John began to grab at straws. "Then what the fuck are you doing here, Liam? Just happened by? I sure as hell didn't call you."

"John, you're smarter than this." Liam shook his head in utter disappointment as he patiently explained, "The newspaper, you moron. Page two, first column. Had a nice picture of your captain and his shiny wings. Want a copy?"

"We've checked that too," the police detective shrewdly interrupted the exchange. "The *Pensacola Post* did run a story about the shooting the morning after, giving Mr. Tasker sufficient time to get here to the hospital."

John felt like the ground had just been pulled out from under him.

Liam did not help secure John's footing as he pleasantly said, "Just wanted to offer a shoulder, John."

"I think I'll snap your neck just on general principle." John pounded his fists on the table, giving his hands something less homicidal to do.

"That's enough!" the police detective warned, just as her radio blared to life.

"Shots fired in ICU!"

Chapter Nine

Swords

Moments before…

Aaron's world spun sickeningly as the bearded man grabbed him by the shoulders and yanked him upright. The pain in his chest stole his breath while the pain in his head stole his thoughts. All in all, it was a useless pile of grayish skin and screaming nerves out of which the man was trying to shake an answer. Aaron managed a chuckle at the fuckwad's efforts.

Another set of hands suddenly gripped his hair and pulled his head back.

"Did you see? Did you see?" A woman's scowl swam before his tearing eyes as she asked over and over, "Did you see?"

Who the hell were these people?

More importantly, where the fuck was John?

The gunshot that followed, Aaron hoped wasn't the answer.

* * *

The conference room was two floors below ICU. John and the detective chose the stairs over waiting for the elevator. Neither spoke as they barreled up the steps.

Despite her training and his exhaustion, John hit the exit door first and tumbled wildly out into the hospital's long hallway. Security was flooding the opposite end of the corridor. John took off at a full run toward the chaos.

Off-duty policemen in polyester uniforms were swarming Aaron's room. Guns were drawn. People were shouting. Monitors were shrilling in alarm.

It was hell, and John couldn't get inside it fast enough.

Shoving his way through, ignoring the detective's demands for him to stop, John finally reached the doorway to Aaron's room and went deathly still. Open-mouthed, he stared.

"What the hell?" the detective at his side voiced the confusion of consensus.

John took in the scene and wholeheartedly agreed.

A stranger with a long, scraggly beard lay sprawled on the floor, obviously dead.

On the bed, Aaron sat awake, a dopey grin on his face and a chokehold on Rose.

And, to top off the madness, Liam Tasker stood in the corner smirking.

Yep. Hell was a good word for it.

* * *

Aaron was moved to a private room. He was checked over from head to toe and back up again by a conglomeration of the hospital's finest doctors. The press had gotten wind of the story, so there was airtime to be won. John let them fight it out for the privilege of a 10:00 news bite. He "no comment"ed himself to death before the staff had secreted them off to another, less accessible corner of the hospital. In the end, all that mattered was that the diagnosis was universally positive. No brain damage. No heart damage. *Just* a broken sternum, a lot of torn muscles, a lot of lost blood and a headache of gargantuan proportion— "gargantuan" being Aaron's word, one of the few he'd actually managed to direct toward John.

Tests, reports, medically dictated and medicinally spurned naps took up most of Aaron's afternoon, leaving John in the background to compose himself.

So by 11:00 that evening, by the time Aaron was tucked nicely into his new bed with knockout medicine in hand, John should have been well prepared to actually talk to his best friend—lover— whatever.

He wasn't.

John sat in the green vinyl chair by Aaron's bedside and twiddled his thumbs.

Aaron, though exhausted and still in considerable pain, lay in his bed wide-eyed and wary. John hadn't said a word to him all evening. "You trying to scare me?" Aaron's voice was tiny, brittle.

John knew better, however; he had tread Aaron's waters before.

"John."

See. There you go. Not a brittle syllable in his whole vocabulary.

"John!" Aaron growled.

Fearing Aaron would next toss an O2 tank at him, John knew his delaying tactic had come to an end. "No." His voice was intentionally flat, devoid of all clues to the sappy mess that was currently molting in his head. "I'm not trying to scare you."

Aaron's sigh was a flimsy excuse for a yawn. "Then what *are* you doing? You're not blaming yourself, are you?"

"Should I?" It was a shitty counter to a man who didn't remember much more than his name.

"No," Aaron sounded so damned sure of himself that John almost believed him. Almost.

"Then I'm not," John lied, with the emotion of a bored rock.

Aaron snorted in a pain-hampered breath. "Just being a bastard, why?"

John took a moment to thank God for poor lighting. Being cloaked in the shadows of nighttime hospital lighting was the only way he was able to cough up, however unattractively, those three little words of infamy and lore: "I love you."

"I know." Aaron yawned.

Thoroughly deflated for only a heartbeat, John quickly gleaned the problem and its solution. Clearing his throat, sitting up straighter in the ugly green chair, still resolutely hiding his eyes in his twiddling thumbs, John Castle proclaimed in a manly squeak, "I'm *in* love with you."

"Figured," Aaron shrugged and chomped lazily on an ice chip.

John counted to ten, twice, before he realized that the bastard's answer was a good one. No further explanation would be needed. No bleeding-heart confessions. No overly romantic shit. "Bastard," slipped out unintentionally.

"That's your job." Aaron put the little paper cup on the metal table. He swung the contraption away with a squeak.

The word "job" suddenly took on a four-letter kind of quality to John. He slumped back down in his chair and said bitterly, "I've been careful. Nobody knows about..." John flapped his hand around, not really knowing how to categorize two fucked-up guys in love.

"Us," Aaron easily solved it all with one softly spoken word. John finally let his eyes find Aaron's. The brown eyes were full of tears, as was the voice. "I wish it didn't matter." Aaron knew the truth as well as John.

Or so Aaron thought. Up to that moment, John had agreed. They couldn't be together without giving up themselves. Aaron's career was his boyhood dream, the skies his true playground. John wouldn't let Aaron give that up for him, but—"One day it won't matter, right?"

"One day?" Aaron repeated slowly, reluctantly allowing a ray of hope to remain.

"Even smart-ass generals retire... one day." John grinned. It was an offer to wait, to hold his own heart in reserve until the skies, one faraway day, let Aaron's go. John hoped he didn't need to say more.

He didn't. Aaron understood the gift he was being given. The brown eyes finally released their tears as a smile slowly took life. "You'll be here?"

"Yep." John dissolved into a smirk. "Right here in this green vinyl chair, or wherever your choice of bed may be."

A weight lifted and disappeared forever from Aaron's soul. The smile turned quickly into a grin. "So, I can go to sleep and you'll…"

"Be here," John vowed.

Just before sleep swept him away, Aaron whispered, "I'm in love with you too."

* * *

Aaron woke once during that night. He looked to his side and found John asleep in the chair. The lights from the parking lot streamed in through the slats of the window's blinds and covered John's face in shadows that brought some disturbing truths home.

John looked terrible, battle-worn and older than his years. Even the flop of hair that usually played mischievously across his brow, now only lay sad and lifeless across his still worry-creased skin. He had to make this man go home and get some real rest.

"John?" Aaron called out in a stage whisper. The last thing he needed was for a nurse to come in and join what he was sure was going to be a fight. Not receiving so much as a twitch in response, Aaron tried again, his tone sharper, "John!"

The man slept on.

Sighing, as his headache was already starting to make a reappearance, Aaron reached over toward the chair, determined to shake the bastard awake.

"Damn!" he cursed as his fingers came just short of John. Still determined, Aaron began to rearrange himself on the bed so he could stretch just those few inches further…

"You'll regret that," A voice stopped him as it

chided from the door. "You'll pull every one of those stitches and then you'll never get John to go home."

Wiser words couldn't have been said, even if they did have to come from the smug lips of Liam Tasker.

Aaron dropped his head wearily back to his pillow and in a low voice asked tiredly, "What are you doing here?" He vaguely remembered seeing Liam in the ICU but had put that hallucination down to a bullet in the head.

"Saving your ass." Liam shrugged off the door's frame and came to the bedside smiling all the way.

"My hero." Aaron snorted as he checked to see that John was still sound asleep. He had no idea what the creep was talking about, but Aaron decided to play along. He didn't need John waking up and going all caveman on him. The idea of John in animal skins might need to be revisited later, but, alas, his prehistoric musings were cruelly interrupted.

"Actually, I came to gloat." Liam parked himself on the side of Aaron's bed, hip on the mattress like he owned it.

"How noble of you." Aaron rolled his eyes.

"The way I hear it, you have me to thank for you and John finally *getting it on*," he mocked with a wink. When Aaron didn't rise to the bait, Liam baited further, "It seems that my little call to you in Colorado opened up a can of worms that you're still fucking to."

Even ignoring the mixed metaphors, Liam's speech was still a crock of shit. "You were being an ass, one of those psycho exes that boil bunnies. You were not trying to be helpful."

"But I ended up being helpful, so I think thanks are in order." Then, leaning in disturbingly close, Liam tossed out what he no doubt thought was his *coup de grace*, "Especially after your *one and only* turned me in to the police for shooting you."

Unfortunately for Mr. Tasker, Aaron's reaction wasn't quite what Liam had hoped. Stitches be damned, Aaron laughed. Hard. With one hand to the hole in his chest, Aaron asked incredulously, "John thought *you* did it? *You*?"

Liam bristled and taunted, "So did the cops, smart ass."

"Good to know." Aaron continued to chuckle as he looked down checking to see if his insides were still inside.

Liam surprised them both by briefly snickering, too. "Yeah, well, my sister would have hacked off my balls if I'd so much as bean with you a beach ball."

"How is she?" Aaron asked with genuine curiosity. "I heard she was going to FSU."

Liam nodded proudly, "A traitor to us all."

Aaron could just imagine the upheaval in the Tasker household when their only girl deserted the family's SEC homeland for an ACC school. A bullet to the head might honestly be less painful. Aaron would know. "But she's healthy?" After all, that was what really mattered.

Liam smiled. "Perfectly."

"Your father?" Aaron had genuinely liked the older gentleman and thought about him often.

Liam seemed surprised by the question but answered with a guarded smile, "He's old, but hanging in there. Keeps wanting to replant that old elm tree in Auburn."

"For God's sakes, why?" That tree still made the occasional appearance in Aaron's nightmares.

"His parents were buried under it, and he keeps talking about moving my mother there... but if he thinks I'm putting him down in that dirt, he's crazy. Now I think the old coot's hanging on just to argue with me about it." Liam grinned grimly.

"Keep arguing." It was all Aaron could think to say.

"Try to stop me."

"And you?" Aaron decided to go for broke.

Liam laughed freely. "Moved on," he waved his left hand complete with gold band Aaron's face, "but still grasping to that old bitterness with every toenail that I've got."

Aaron was impressed. It took real balls to admit to being a weasel. As for the married thing, he wasn't surprised. Of all people, Aaron understood the pull of both sexes, but the question still remained: "Why *are* you here?"

Liam rolled out his best smirk. "Heard what happened, wanted to see if there was room to move in."

Aaron snorted. "Same old bastard."

"Yep." Liam patted Aaron gently on the knee as he stood up to leave. "Just watch your step with John. I'll be watching."

"Like the buzzard that you are." Amused, Aaron shook his head.

Liam laughed, gave John one last lingering look, and walked out the door.

"I'm not going home," a groggy but perfectly functional John immediately notified his lover from his much beloved green vinyl chair.

"You stink," Aaron politely pointed out. He even scrunched up his nose to aid in the deception.

"Probably your stupid coat," John countered as he removed the leather jacket from its latest job as lap blanket.

Aaron squinted into the darkened corner that held his best friend, not sure how that coat had made it here. "Why is..."

"It doesn't matter." John waved him off not wanting to revisit those circumstances tonight. Folding the coat neatly, he placed it again on his lap. He stared at it as he spoke softly, "For nine years I've been meaning to ask you..." Instead of using words John just fingered the mended bullet hole that lay neatly across the coat's chest and waited for an answer.

Aaron didn't understand why it seemed so important to John, but he replied in the same solemn tone, "My father was wearing it when he was shot down in Korea. My mother was his nurse, and she patched it up for him." A small smile of remembrance brushed Aaron's lips. "And that's how their story started. Guess that's why she wanted him to be buried in it."

"And why you *couldn't* let him be buried in it," John surmised.

"Yeah." The look of contentment grew into concern as he watched John fidget with the jacket.

"Kind of weird, both you and him..." John drifted off as he kept running his fingers over the coat's scar. "Well, you were naked, so I can't exactly patch up your clothes, but..." Again, he drifted away, letting Aaron glean any wayward meaning for himself. "Well, you get the idea."

Aaron certainly did. "Come here." He patted the space on the bed beside him.

John looked pointedly at the open door.

Aaron shrugged. "We'll blame Liam." When that didn't immediately work, Aaron relented, "Please."

"You said I stunk," John grumbled but, nonetheless, rose from the chair.

"You do." Aaron continued to inch carefully over. Once he was as far over as his shaky body could manage, he gave John the all clear. "No hanky panky."

John snorted as he settled in. "Don't worry. My hanky's in no condition to be messing with your panky."

"What happened to your hand?" The whiteness of John's bandage stood out in stark contrast to the overall grunge of the rest of the doctor. Aaron didn't know how he'd missed it before.

Hiding the appendage under the blanket, John's shoulders slumped as he sorrowfully confessed, "I pulled a *you*. Got mad. Put a hole in a window. No big deal."

Aaron replied with a sleepy chuckle, "I'll remember that when I get mad at one of your windows."

After much gentle maneuvering on Aaron's part and a careful avoidance of all stitched areas by John, the doctor diagnosed with one leg still dangling from the bed, "This is damned uncomfortable."

"Yeah." Aaron laid his gently on John's shoulder and snuggled in with a long, soft sigh.

Looking down at the love of his life once again loving his life, John swore with all of his suddenly sap-laden heart, "I'm never moving."

"Never." With a jaw-breaking yawn, Aaron concurred.

* * *

"Explain it to me again." Whatever drugs they were giving him sure weren't helping Aaron's memory. The "incident" in ICU had happened two days ago, and Aaron was still asking for broad clarifications—any broader and John would be spelling out Aaron's name. In crayon.

"Want me to use finger-puppets this time?"

Aaron lit up like a light bulb. "I want to be the thumb!"

"Yep." John reached for the call button. "Enough *everything* for you." Going through a couple of bullet wounds cold turkey couldn't be as annoying as this.

Aaron grabbed his arm and smiled a real, honestly coherent smile. "Kidding."

John eyed him down like a perp in a cop show line-up. He passed muster, barely. John slowly retreated back to his green vinyl chair.

Aaron chuckled before settling back into simple honesty, "It's like I'm swimming in molasses, here. Just tell me the story again, slowly, okay?"

"Okay." John almost had the tale down by rote. "Nathan Hyland, the old man with the beard, is the one who shot you."

"At first, I thought he was our 'bearded one' from Chicago. How messed up would that have been?"

"Well, it wasn't him. It was Nathan Hyland."

"Nathan Hyland smells like tuna fish?"

For the hundredth time, John answered in waning patience, "There was no tuna fish. There never was any tuna fish. The tuna fish is just your subconscious's way of laughing at you."

Aaron stuck out his lower lip and pouted.

John laughed. Nobody had ever made him laugh the way Aaron did every single day. "If I had lost you, I…" He broke off when his eyes suddenly began to tear. He had to get Aaron out of this fucking hospital before John dissolved into a permanent mound of mush.

Aaron snorted. "If you had lost me, you'd have been just a grumpy old man living in a yellow house." For some inexplicable reason, the very idea of Dr. John Castle living in a sunshine-hued cottage by the sea had always tickled Aaron. "Now, with me alive and kicking, you're going to be a grumpy old man with a hot boyfriend living in a yellow house."

"Point." John smiled as he borrowed one of Aaron's favorite expressions. "Now, where was I?"

"Tuna fish."

"No more talking," John immediately warned. A deep breath was taken, a prayer for patience was made, and John began again. "Hyland, the bearded guy, was certifiably crazy. He'd been in the hospital for a check-up when he met Olive Simms." At Aaron's scrunched-up face, John explained softly, "She's the woman I lost in surgery the day you were shot." Another deep breath, and John dove back in refreshed. "Apparently, Hyland had just met her in passing but had somehow associated her with his own daughter, a woman who had died a year ago. Still at the hospital, he heard what happened to Olive. He went crazier. He wanted revenge." Deep breath number three. He'd blame himself once he had Aaron at 100%. Until then, John just wanted to get this over with. "So, Hyland checked himself out, found out where I lived, hung out in your rose bushes and watched us fuck."

For a man who had lost an ungodly amount of blood, Aaron still managed to pale further. "He watched the whole thing?"

John rolled his eyes. Of all the things to worry about, only his pilot would pick that. "Yes, the whole thing. I guess, we fascinated him." It was Aaron's turn to roll his eyes. John continued, "Hyland decided taking you out would hurt me more than blowing my brains across the patio." John gave up a sheepish smile. "The bastard was right."

John watched the cogs churn slowly in Aaron's medicated head. Finally, Aaron nodded and asked, "So where does that woman I had the headlock on come in?"

"Rose Van den Burgh." Even her name gave John a bad taste of betrayal. "She and Hyland were long time lovers. He told her what he'd done and instead of turning his ass in, she decided to aid and abet." Nope, no bitterness here. "Since she worked here, she used her seniority to get assigned to your case. She needed to know what we knew, such as if anybody saw Hyland that night at my house. I had already let it slip that I hadn't, so she just needed to know if you had."

The manic *"Did you see? Did you see?"* came quickly back to Aaron's mind. "And if I had seen?"

There were certain things John refused to think about. That was one of them. "I don't know what she planned to do. Apparently Hyland didn't know either. So when he brought Rose her lunch that afternoon, he brought the gun too. I guess, he decided to take care of you himself." John paled this time.

"And?" After a minute, Aaron urged him on softly.

John sighed and rushed on, "When they couldn't get a straight answer out of you, Hyland took a shot. She claims she hit his gun hand on purpose, but who knows?" John doubted everything that bitch said. "Anyhow, he missed. A guard who had heard the shot came in and killed Hyland when he wouldn't put the gun down. Rose cracked, tried to jump for Hyland's gun, but you didn't let her get there. Pretty impressive chokehold for an ICU kid." The doctors had in fact been amazed at Aaron's ability to reason and act on that reasoning while being doped up to the gills. The whole thing just made John want to hurl.

Aaron rubbed his head and nodded slowly, "And that's it?"

John wished. "Oh, Liam was there. He knew this place and took the closer stairs from the conference room getting to the ICU before me. While the guard was holding his gun on Rose, Liam kicked Hyland's gun out of reach, and then he just stood back and watched you in action."

"My hero," Aaron repeated his words from their conversation with a shake of his head and a smirk. "Maybe he's the one that smelled like tuna fish? You used to fuck the guy, he ever get a tuna fishy smell about him? Maybe a seafood-scented sweat...?"

John kissed Aaron soundly to shut him up.

* * *

Aaron would come to refer to her as simply "Ma Barker." She didn't deserve any derivative of Ro's name, the pilot would explain in his more somber moments. Besides, it added some much needed color to the ICU room "shootout." Being targeted by a gun-toting grandma head over heels in love with a crazy old man just didn't have the same zing as Ma Barker protecting her brood. Either way, Aaron tended to put a kinder spin to his assailant's motives than the actions truly dictated. He could understand where she was coming from, although he admitted her chosen path had seesawed between squirrelly and outright demented.

John was not nearly as forgiving. He always called by her full name, Rose Van den Burgh, like people do with serial killers. He attended every day of her trial and sentencing, and learned that Hyland had brought her a tuna fish sandwich for her lunch that day—a fact John was never, ever going to share with Aaron. Aaron was wonderfully insufferable enough.

Rose Van den Burgh pled guilty by reason of mental defect, so the court days were filled with the psychiatric communities' endorsements and damnations of the rehabilitation of the criminally insane. John didn't care what they did with her, as long as she was behind lock and key. In the end, her cell was padded and her days filled with heavy medication and group therapy. No one ever visited her, and John thought that was the cruelest and most deserving punishment of all.

Her lover was buried beside his daughter, with the words "Forgive him" engraved on his simple marker.

Aaron did. John didn't. No real surprise there.

The stunner came six months later when there was a banging at John's front door. He still lived in the same yellow house a few steps from the Gulf. Aaron refused to let him give up his dream place for something as trivial as a "mob hit." John reluctantly agreed as long as Aaron agreed not to put up a tacky plaque memorializing the spot of "the brave Captain Chambers' ruthless gunning down." Aaron agreed quickly, picturing something more in the lines of a statue to commemorate the spot—a plan Aaron kept on the back burner for now.

It was noon, it was absurdly hot, and John had just fixed himself a peanut butter and jelly sandwich. He opened the door with his lunch in hand.

Aaron stood on his doorstep in his full Air Force dress blues. The goofy grin on his face lessened the effect of the big sword on his hip.

Barefoot, in Bermuda shorts and a ripped T-shirt emblazoned with "Spring Break '96," John wiped a smudge of peanut butter off of his face. "Who died?" he asked with a smart-ass smirk.

"Do you care?" Aaron returned the cocky smirk, knowing just how enthusiastically his dress blues affected John's baser needs.

"As long as it's not you, no." John stepped back to let Aaron and his regalia inside and away from prying eyes. His neighbors had gotten noticeably nosier since the late night shooting. John completely understood, but it could get tiring when you're trying to fly low of the "Don't Ask, Don't Tell" idiocy of the military. "Hurry up, sword-master." He always thought the sword was a bit over the top, but he couldn't deny its certain carnal appeal. John stopped when he saw Aaron wasn't budging. "Come on!"

Aaron stubbornly shook his head.

John was tired, he was hot, he was hungry, but he decided to play along. "So you've decided to out yourself on my front door step…while wearing a sword? How visual of you."

"Smart ass."

"I believe I called *you* that on the day we met."

Aaron was truly surprised. "You remember that?"

"I do." John let the two words stand alone for just a moment before adding, "For a while there, memory lane was a hell of a better place to be than…" John saw no need in finishing that statement.

Neither did Aaron. "Point." He nodded firmly in concession.

"So are you going to tell me why you and your shiny sword are loitering on my doorstep?" It was a simple enough question, one that would surely get them into the air-conditioned house right away.

Aaron had other plans. "You're eating a peanut butter sandwich," he accused, a look of disgust on his face as John licked off a spot of jam from his thumb.

John had long since learned that following one of Aaron's tangents was a hell of a lot easier than reining one back. John shrugged and took another bite. "And jelly. So?"

Aaron looked truly peeved. Readjusting his sword angrily, the pilot explained with a sigh of utter exasperation, "I just never pictured myself proposing to a man with peanut butter breath."

John was struck dumb.

Aaron took that as a cue to ramble on. "I mean, I get all gussied up in this infernally hot suit and risk filleting myself with this damn sword on my way over here only to find you barefoot and eating peanut butter. What's wrong with this picture?"

John couldn't utter a word. He just stood there

with his mouth open, half-eaten sandwich in hand, and listened.

"I'll tell you what's wrong with it. I hate peanut butter. You know I hate peanut butter. And yet you're eating peanut butter at the moment I'm either dying and kissing you goodbye, or dying and kissing you as my husband-to-be. Either way...yuck."

John dropped the sandwich.

"Better. But I'm not cleaning it up. And if you don't hurry up and answer me, I'm taking this fucking suit off anyway. I just resigned, and I'm not planning on putting this thing on ever again."

John finally found his tongue and stammered out the only that really mattered, "What about the sword?" After all, the rest they could just make up along the way.

Aaron smiled one of those smiles as he bargained mischievously, "If you say yes, I'll wear it for your birthdays."

"Yes." As if there was ever any doubt. John Castle grabbed Aaron Chambers by his dress blues and pulled him in for a mind-blowing kiss right there for the entire world to see.

Several minutes later, a puffy lipped pilot cocked his head to the side and asked his doctor, "It was the sword, wasn't it?"

John grinned. "No, it was the man."

About the Author

Chloe Stowe is the author of 17 romance novels. Chloe enjoys weaving humor into her action-packed stories of love and life. A quirky character herself, whose daily battles with a chronic panic disorder has filled her daily writing blog for the last three years, Chloe adores odd souls with flawed but fevered hearts. A full-time writer who has earned her Masters in Art History from FSU, she is most proud of being a survivor.

www.chloestowe.com

Excerpt from *Forever Bound with Tinsel*

Chapter One

The basketball flew through the December air with a silent grace, hit the rim of the goal with a *clank!* and took out an elf in the rose bushes with a "crash!" followed directly by a "Damn!"

The *damn!* was provided by John Castle.

The droll condemnation of "Well, you killed him," which immediately followed, came from his lover, best friend and would-be next victim, Aaron Chambers. Aaron stood with his arms crossed against his heaving chest, legs shoulder width apart and a look of betrayal etched across his handsome though frowning face.

John had had just about enough of this shit. "It's an elf!" he defended in a growl. Stomping over to the crime scene, he bent down and picked up the merrily painted though headless corpse. He held it out to his partner by its curly-toed shoes. "You've brought, what, three hundred of these over here the last couple of weeks? I think the colony will survive."

"The question is quickly becoming: will you?" Aaron rebutted with a cocky-ass grin.

If Aaron wasn't basically dripping with sex right now, John would have taken the pilot's ego down a few dozen notches. As it was, however, John was more interested in what the bastard was wearing than what crap was spouting from those thoroughly edible lips.

Aaron's white t-shirt was currently soaked with sweat, the cotton clinging to him like some kind of pornographic lichen. The light gray sweatpants were hardly any better for John's concentration. The paper-thin material sat low on narrow hips and greedily cradled Aaron's substantial assets with X-rated abandon.

The SOB shimmied just enough to twitch John's keen-eyed dick.

"I saw that," the pilot singsonged.

"If we had the time, you'd feel it," the doctor sweetly vowed.

Tyndall Air Force Base's annual Christmas Ball loomed only hours away. It was the region's premier charity event of the year. All the top military brass and all the top hospital patrons would be there, which unfortunately meant so would John and Aaron.

Aaron's rank of colonel and his highly prized position as an instructor in Tyndall's flight school gave the Air Force pilot little choice but to attend. The military was nothing if not political.

John's position as head orthopedic surgeon at Bay Medical Hospital dictated his presence as well.

If only they could have gone together as the couple they were, everything would have been merry and bright on this December 23. Unfortunately the military's Don't Ask, Don't Tell policy played the idiotic Grinch in this feature. DADT was a mealy-mouthed creature with no heart but an ass big enough to literally squash a soldier's career. Because of this policy, John and Aaron had been forced to keep their true relationship a secret from everyone. The world knew them as longtime best friends, only the heavens and their hearts knew them as the soul mates they were.

Aaron was willing to give up his career for John.

John wasn't. He would never be able to live with himself if he was the cause of Aaron's childhood dreams being grounded. Aaron's father had been an Air Force pilot, and all the young man had ever wanted in his life was to be just like his dad. The doctor, no matter how much he wanted to shout to the world that Aaron Chambers was his, couldn't take that away from him.

So John vowed to wait.

And Aaron vowed to hurry... at least as much as a man in the service can hurry a career. Aaron lived with both guilt and gratitude every day.

John knew this and, in turn, latched on to a chunk of guilt all for himself.

Around and around the guilt went, never stopping.

The blame, however, was laid solely on one Grinch's doorstep... Don't Ask, Don't Tell.

Speaking of which...

"I'm thinking of screwing you under one of the generals' tables tonight." Setting the headless body up against the house next to about a dozen other such elfin atrocities, John turned back around with a grin. "So, you game?"

"No." Aaron had recovered the basketball and now dribbled it slowly from hand to hand as he stood there looking fuckable.

"Your cock says otherwise," John singsonged.

Aaron looked down at his pants and rolled his eyes when he found them tented. Tucking the ball under an armpit, he pointed angrily at John. "I blame you for this."

"I would hope so." John thought it only proper to be smug.

Aaron rolled his eyes, dropped the basketball and sat his ass down on it. Everything but his smirk looked tired. "You know, I didn't used to be so…"

John dropped down on the pavement in front of him, legs splayed on either side of his lover. "Adventuresome? Brave? Self-assured and cocky?" He put a little twang on the last just to bug Aaron even more.

Shaking his head, Aaron snorted. "I was going to say stupid and horny…"

"Well, that too." John shrugged, amenable to just about anything that meant there was going to be hot and sticky sex, sooner rather than later. Four hours was plenty of time to kill off a few more brain cells with a mind-blowing orgasm or two. Santa would understand them being a little late. After all, it was the old guy who'd come up with the naughty list in the first place.

Sometimes it was scary how Aaron could read John's mind. This, unfortunately, was one of those times. Narrowing his eyes, Aaron snapped, "Don't sit there looking all innocent and wholesome. You're an elf killer… an elf killer at Christmas, no less! Santa's going to enjoy mowing your ass down with his sleigh."

"How old are you again?" It was a common question, one John could now say in three languages.

Aaron had opened his mouth to, no doubt, say something biting or wicked or both when a car suddenly backfired down the street.

Briefly Aaron appeared startled. Nothing more.

John, however, was more. Much more.

Other Riverdale Avenue Books Titles You Might Enjoy

Forever Bound with Tinsel
By Chloe Stowe

Fangsters: Clan of the Jersey Boys
By Ryan Field

Fangsters 2: Gangbang Fangsters
By Ryan Field

Valley of the Dudes
By Ryan Field

Stepbrothers in the Attic
By Ryan Field

50 Shades of Gay
By Jeffery Self

The Hunger Gays
By Nathan Alexander